Q

What does
**PALMTOP
TIGER**
mean to you?

Toradora!

Yuyuko Takemiya
Illustrations: Yasu

♪ Being persistent
is the only merit this kid has
'cause Minorin believes in him!
Zoo da da da da dee din! ♪

Oh! Yeah!

...Those are all
the lyrics I could
come up with.

Kushieda Minori ✳ ✳
Always smiling and doing things her own
way, she makes the world around her all
the more fun and inviting with her whimsi-
cal behavior. President of the girls' softball
club, this airhead is also the only one who
can control the "Palmtop Tiger."

Right after getting out of the north exit ticket gates, take a left, and go straight 200 meters! I'm the Bishamon bar's Mirano-chan! How old do you think I am? Twenty-three? That's right! As a freebie for getting it right...you get one beer on the house! Come play any time!

Umm...

Ahhh! Ryu-chan, did you seeee? Today, I'm not coming home until around four, okay?

Takasu Yasuko ✳ ✳ ✳

Her alias is Mirano, forever twenty-three years old. At the two-person Takasu household, she's dependent on the serious Ryuuji, but on the battle-field (also called the bar) she works spectacularly hard...sometimes.

To ra do ra ♪

VOLUME 1

story Yuyuko Takemiya • *illustrations* Yasu

...In the end, no one understands me anyway.

Aisaka Taiga
★ THE
PALMTOP TIGER
★

This is a story concerning that "Palmtop Tiger."
A story of love and harmony...

Toradora!

In this world, there's something that no one
has ever seen.
Something gentle, and oh-so-sweet.
If anyone ever saw it, they'd surely want it
for themselves.
But that's precisely why no one's ever seen it.
In order to keep it safe, the world hid it away.
But someday, someone will find it.
Only the one who was meant to have it will
find it, in the end.

That's how it's meant to be.

TORADORA! Vol. 1

Edited by ASCII MEDIA WORKS.
First published in Japan in 2006 by KADOKAWA
CORPORATION, Tokyo. English translation rights arranged
with KADOKAWA CORPORATION, Tokyo.

Follow Seven Seas Entertainment online at
sevenseasentertainment.com.

TRANSLATION: Jan Cash & Vincent Castaneda
ADAPTATION: J.P. Sullivan
COPY EDITING: Marykate Jasper
COVER DESIGN: Nicky Lim
INTERIOR LAYOUT & DESIGN: Clay Gardner
PROOFREADER: Jade Gardner, Stephanie Cohen
LIGHT NOVEL EDITOR: Jenn Grunigen
PRODUCTION ASSISTANT: CK Russell
PRODUCTION MANAGER: Lissa Pattillo
EDITOR-IN-CHIEF: Adam Arnold
PUBLISHER: Jason DeAngelis

ISBN: 978-1-626927-95-7
Printed in Canada
First Printing: May 2018
10 9 8 7 6 5 4 3 2 1

BY
Yuyuko Takemiya

ILLUSTRATED BY
Yasu

Seven Seas Entertainment

ToC
Table of Contents

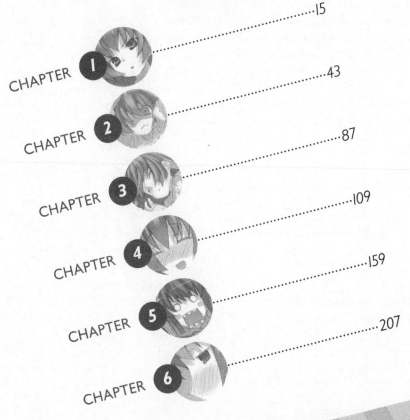

CHAPTER **1** 15

CHAPTER **2** 43

CHAPTER **3** 87

CHAPTER **4** 109

CHAPTER **5** 159

CHAPTER **6** 207

"**...D**AMN IT."

It was 7:30 AM in the morning. The weather was fair, but the room was dark.

He was on the second floor of a wood-walled, two-story rental. The south-facing, two-bedroom apartment was a ten-minute walk from a private rail station. The rent: 80,000 yen.

"I give up. This is useless."

Resigning himself to his annoyance, he vigorously rubbed a fogged-up mirror with the palm of his hand. The shabby bathroom was still humid from the shower he'd taken that morning, so the mirror quickly clouded over again, right where he'd just wiped it.

But it wasn't the mirror he was annoyed at.

"What bogus advice."

"Soft bangs for a softer look!"—those words had frolicked on the pages of a style magazine catering to current male fashion trends.

Takasu Ryuuji's bangs were definitely "soft" right then. Just like the article instructed, he'd pulled his hair all the way out, used a dryer at full blast to make the bangs naturally stand on end, and then worked them to the sides with a light-hold hair wax. He had done everything—everything—just as the article said in order to get it looking exactly like the model's hair. All that work was the product of waking up thirty minutes early in the hopes of fulfilling his desire.

All that work—for nothing.

"It's not as if I'll really change just from doing my bangs," he said. "That was probably wishful thinking..."

He took that effeminate magazine, the one that he'd swallowed his pride to buy, and half-heartedly tossed it at the waste bin. He cringed—a miss. The bin toppled and spewed out its contents, and the magazine he'd just discarded flopped open to a page of fashion tips, laying there amidst the trash.

It read, "Soft or Wild?! What you can still do to declare your transformation for the new school year! Our authoritative guide to your debut!" If he could say one thing in response to that, it would be that he never wanted a "debut."

But he *did* want a transformation. Yet it had ended in failure.

Out of complete desperation, he used a wetted hand to muss the softened bangs he'd just spent so much effort making until they reverted back to his usual straight hairstyle. Then he kneeled on the floor to gather the trash.

"Wha—?! Wh-what is this...? There's mold... it's growing mold *again*?!"

He'd discovered black mold along the wooden baseboard near the bath.

There was mold, even though he was always careful to wipe away excess moisture. Just the previous week, he'd held a mold-cleaning rally (a competition for all things water-related) for a whole day. Apparently, not even that level of effort could vanquish the run-down house's poor ventilation. He bit his thin lips in frustration, and as a last-ditch effort, tried scrubbing the mold with a tissue. Naturally, it didn't come off; the tissue just came apart in bits that added even more mess. An exercise in futility.

"Damn it... I just used the last of the mold remover, too. I'll have to buy more again..."

Right, then. He couldn't do anything but leave it as it was. *I'll destroy you for sure*, he thought, fixing the mold with a sidelong glare while he cleaned up the scattered trash. He took the opportunity to give the floor a cursory wipe with the tissue. After disposing of the fallen hair and dust, he wiped all the moisture from the washbasin, lifted his head, and finally took a deep breath.

"Whew. That's right, I need to feed her... Inko-chan!"

"Yahh!"

A shrill reply returned the high school boy's rough call. Good, she was awake.

After regaining his composure, he entered the wood-floored kitchen, still barefoot. He prepared the feed and a change of newspaper, then headed to the tatami mat living room. He removed the cloth covering the birdcage filling one corner of the room and was thus reunited with his beloved pet, whom he hadn't seen since the night before. He didn't know what other owners did, but at the Takasu household, that was how they took care of Inko.

When sleeping, her face was downright unpleasant, so they hid her until she woke in the morning.

"Inko-chan, good morning."

Inko-chan was an inko—a yellow parakeet. He spoke to her while replenishing her feed, as usual.

"G-good... good morn..." Although her eyebrows twitched creepily—like she didn't even understand what she was saying— the ever-clever Inko-chan managed to answer in Japanese. She'd just woken up, but she was in high spirits. This side of her was a little cute, he had to admit.

"Inko-chan, say thank you for the food."

"Thank—ank—you—thank you for the food! Thank you for the food! Thank! You!"

"That's it, that'll do. Okay, let's see if you can say *that* today. Can you say your own name? Say 'Inko-chan.'"

"I-In-Ini-In-nnn... Inn." Summoning all the strength in her body, Inko-chan waved her head, contorted her posture, and jerkily swung open her wings.

"Iii..." Her eyes narrowed, and her ashen tongue peeked out from her beak. Today might be it—her owner clenched his fists. But...

"...Iiidiot."

Ah, the intelligence of birds. As expected of a one-gram brain.

With a sigh, he gathered up the dirtied newspaper into a plastic bag. But as he consolidated it with the rest of the trash and prepared to head to the kitchen, he heard something.

"Where're ya goin'?"

It was coming from behind the sliding door, barely ajar. It seemed the *other* idiot had woken up.

"Ryu-chan, whaddya wearin' your uniform for...?"

He quickly closed the trash bag and turned to the owner of the voice. "I'm going to school. I told you yesterday that today was the start of the school year, didn't I?"

"Ohhh... Then... then..." Sprawled on the futon, she spoke as if on the verge of tears. "Then, what about my lunch...? What about my bento...? I can't smell that bento smell! Ryu-chan, didn't you make me one?"

"Nope."

"Wahhh! What'll I do when I wake up? There's nothing to eat!"

"I'll be home before you're awake. Today's just the opening ceremonies."

"Oh...that's all, huh?" She laughed, knocking her feet together. *Clap clap clap clap*! She used her feet to give him a standing ovation...or maybe a sprawling ovation.

"The opening ceremony, huh? Congratulations! That means you're a second-year student, starting today."

"Never mind that. Didn't I tell you to at least wipe off your makeup before bed? You kept saying it was too much trouble, so I even bought you those easy-cleaning wipes... Argh, there's foundation all over the pillowcase again! This stuff doesn't come out in the wash, you know! And who knows what'll happen to your skin—you're old enough to know better."

"Sorrryyyy."

She got up as-is, fully exposing her leopard print panties, large chest jiggling. Wavy, mostly-blonde hair fell across the valley of her chest in a tangled, disheveled mess. She oozed "femininity" as she brushed up that hair with her long-nailed hands.

But then she said, "I drank so much that I only got home an hour ago... Sooo sleeeepy... *Yaaawn*... Oh, right... I brought back pudding!"

While yawning, she rubbed her mascara-laden eyes, then crawled toward the convenience store bag she'd unceremoniously dumped in a corner of the room. Those manners, that puckered mouth, the mumbling of *pudding, pudding*, her plump cheeks, her round eyes—it was all embarrassingly childish.

This strange woman, who many might call a beauty...

"Huh? Ryu-chaan, I can't find the spoon!"

"The clerk probably forgot to put one in."

"Nu-uh, I'm sure I saw him do it... Huh..."

She was, in fact, Takasu Ryuuji's biological mother: Takasu Yasuko (alias Mirano), thirty-three years old (but eternally claiming twenty-three). She worked as an entertainer at the town's one and only hostess bar, Bishamon Heaven.

Yasuko inverted the bag, rummaged around the corner of the futon, and tilted her small face in disappointment.

"The room's so dark... No way can I find it like this. Ryu-chaan, can you open the curtains a little?"

"They are open."

"Whaa? Ohh, right. I forgot since I'm usually not awake at this time..."

In the dim room, the mismatched parent and child both breathed a small sigh.

Their apartment had one large, south-facing window. In the six years since they started renting it, they'd come to completely depend on the bright sunlight that flooded in from the south.

With their entryway on the north side and neighboring buildings to the east and west spaced just dozens of centimeters away, they only had southern-facing windows. Since the apartment got such amazing natural sunlight, they hadn't needed to turn on the overheads from sunrise to sunset. The morning rays were particularly strong; rainy days excepted, they lavished illumination upon Ryuuji when he made their lunches and also on Yasuko, while she slept out of exhaustion.

"Sure is a huge condo, isn't it...?" she said.

"I wonder what kind of people live there... Should I turn on the light?" Ryuuji asked.

Last year, a ten-story, ultra-high-end luxury condo went up just a few meters from their apartment's south window. Naturally, the sunlight stopped coming in, which tormented him with all kinds of maddening frustration. First, the laundry wouldn't dry. Then the corners of the tatami mats swelled and bubbled with moisture. Mold had started growing, and the condensation was terrible. The wallpaper's peeling edges were no doubt owed to the moisture, as well. Ryuuji tried telling himself to calm down, since it was just a rental, but he was a high-strung guy. He couldn't help but find such unsanitary living conditions intolerable.

Now, the two of them could only peer open-mouthed at the white bricks of that luxury condo, bound together in squalor.

"Wellll, it's probably fine," Yasuko said. "I sleep right through the mornings, anyhow."

"Complaining about it won't change anything, either...and hey, the rent did go down by five thousand yen," he said, as he brought Yasuko a spoon from the kitchen. Ryuuji scratched his head. This was no time to have a family moment. It was nearly time for him to leave.

After throwing his randoseru backpack on, he stooped down from his newly grown-up height to put on socks. Then, once he made sure he had everything he needed, he noticed the slight throbbing in his chest.

That's right, he thought, remembering again. *Today is the first day of the new school year*. Opening ceremonies first, and after that—the class assignments.

He'd failed to change his image, but that didn't mean he was depressed. A faint feeling of hope, or anticipation, or something along those lines, fluttered in Ryuuji's stomach, even if he wasn't the type to show it on his face.

"...I'm off. Remember to lock the doors and change out of your pajamas."

"Yuuup. Oh, hey, Ryu-chan, hey." Still sprawled on her futon, Yasuko bit down on her spoon with her back teeth and smiled like a kid. "Ryu-chan, you're kinda looking fired up! You'd better do your best as a second-year student! You're going places I never got to."

Yasuko had dropped out of school as a first-year in order to have Ryuuji, and so she didn't know anything about the world of a second-year high school student. For a moment, Ryuuji started feeling sentimental. "I guess so."

He smiled a little and raised a hand. It was his way of showing gratitude towards his mother, but it backfired. Yasuko let out a squeal and rolled around enthusiastically—then she said it. She said *that*.

"Ryu-chan, you're so *cool*! Every day, you look more like your daddy!"

"Tch!"

...She'd said it.

Ryuuji mutely closed the front door, and then instinctively looked up at the sky. His vision spun around and around; he felt as though a deep whirlpool surrounded his feet, drawing him downwards. He hated it. *No,* he thought, *no, stop it.*

That was the one phrase he never, ever wanted *anyone* to say to him.

Especially on a day like today.

You look like your daddy.

It seemed Yasuko couldn't understand how much that fact troubled Ryuuji. It was the whole reason he bought that magazine and tried out softer bangs.

On the way to school, Ryuuji's face twisted into a sullen expression. His high school was well within walking distance of their house, but he still moved at a fast clip, taking long, straight strides.

He sighed and unconsciously pulled on his bangs. He hid his eyes out of habit. Yes, his troubles lay in his eyes.

They were *bad.*

It had nothing to do with his eyesight.

It was the way they looked.

Though his facial features had rapidly grown more masculine in the past year, that hadn't made him extraordinarily handsome, or given him out-of-this-world good looks. Well, he wasn't *bad*-looking, either... Not that anyone would say that out loud—but he thought he didn't look too bad, at least.

His eyes were appalling, though. They were so awful, there was no way he would ever be considered handsome.

He had angular sanpaku eyes. The kind of eyes ringed by white on all sides. On top of that, his eyeballs themselves were huge; the blue-tinged whites threw off an intense, garish light. His dim, small black irises moved swiftly, as if trying to cut straight through whatever was unfortunate enough to be the target of their gaze. Despite Ryuuji's intentions, his eyes seemed to possess the ability to strike panic into anyone that saw them... He understood that. He understood it all too well. It was so bad that even *he* had become flustered after seeing a kid with an absolutely livid expression in a group photo—until realizing he was looking at himself.

It wasn't just his eyes, though. Thanks to his curt personality, his way of speaking probably also came off a little rough. Sometimes he got high-strung, too. More than that, though, was the fact that he was the type of person who struggled with the fine line between jokes and sarcasm. Because he lived alone with a woman like Yasuko, he'd probably also lost any innocence or meekness he once had... Really, he considered himself the real parent out of the two of them.

But even so, scenes like these kept happening...

"Wh-what, Takasu? Are you disobeying a teacher?! S-someone hold him back! Hold him back!"

You're mistaken. I forgot about part of the presentation, so I just came to apologize.

"S-s-s-s-sorry, it wasn't on purpose, I bumped into you because he p-p-p-pushed me."

Who would get angry from just being brushed on the shoulder?

"I heard that damn Takasu guy crashed another school's graduation in junior high and holed himself up in their announcement room."

I'm not that bad an apple.

"...I guess I should start being more proactive about clearing up misunderstandings," Ryuuji said, sighing at the bitter memories he'd unearthed.

His grades weren't bad. He was never late or absent. He'd never hit anyone—he'd never even had a heated argument with anyone before. Long story short, Takasu Ryuuji was a very ordinary young man. But, simply because he had a fearsome look in his eyes (and maybe because his only parent was in the bar business), everyone believed he was a terrible delinquent.

If anyone stayed in the same class with him for a year, those stupid misunderstandings would eventually be resolved. But a year wasn't short, especially not to a high school student, and today he would have to start all over again. On top of all that, his attempted image change had been a failure.

Nonetheless, he looked forward to the class rotation. There was someone in particular he wanted to share a class with. But when his thoughts started running through the hardships that lay ahead, his hopes seemed to whiz away and deflate to half their size.

It was all because of that unwelcome comment Yasuko had made... No, that wasn't right. It was all because of the unwelcome genes branded into him by his father.

"Your daddy's in heaven, now. He was so cool—he had a coif with shaved sides, and he wore these really pointy patent leather shoes that he always shined... And on his neck, he had a gold chain, like thiiiis thick, and a baggy suit, and a Rolex. Oh, and he always layered a weekly magazine over his stomach. When I asked him what that was for, he said it was so he'd be safe if he ever got stabbed. Ahhh! He was so *exciting*."

He remembered Yasuko's enchanted expression when she recounted all that. Afterwards, she'd shown him the only picture left of his father.

His father looked exactly as Yasuko described.

He stood posed with his legs spread arrogantly wide. He had a carrying case under his arm. He wore a white suit with an incredibly showy open-neck shirt, several gold rings glinted on both his hands, and a diamond stud adorned one ear. His lower jaw was thrust out, as though jeering towards the camera. One of his hands groped at the breast of a younger version of Ryuuji's mother. She held an enlarged stomach, and her carefree laugh was almost audible from the picture: "Ha ha!" His father's front teeth were gold.

He was really kind, and sincere, and never raised his hand against a civilian even once, and on and on Yasuko would go. Yet, a person who was kind and sincere wouldn't join the yakuza to become a mobster, nor would they get what had likely been a much younger high school student pregnant. Beyond all that, however, were those sharp eyes of his.

They were eyes that would make you drop your wallet without a fuss if ever they stared straight at you. Just his gaze by itself threatened unreasonable violence. An unpleasant thought had risen to Ryuuji's mind: *That same look is stuck on my face...*

Ordering people not to get the wrong idea was probably impossible. After all, even *Ryuuji* imagined his father as a scary man, and he had no memory of him.

All that said, his father was probably still alive. According to Yasuko, he'd been turned into Swiss cheese while saving an underling and had been dumped into a Yokohama harbor somewhere—but there was no grave. There was also no memorial shrine. There were no ashes or earthly possessions left behind, or Buddhist tablets, either. Ryuuji had no memory of any of that happening. And when Yasuko was drunk, she would sometimes put on a sly smile and say, "If daddy suddenly came home, what would Ryuu-chan doooo? Hee hee hee hee, I wonder."

Ryuuji's father was probably serving time behind cold iron bars. That was what his son thought.

"Yo, Takasu! Morning—sure is a nice day!"

Ryuuji noticed the voice behind him and turned around to raise his hand. "Yo, Kitamura. Morning."

There's no helping it, Ryuuji thought, as he stopped to wait for Kitamura Yuusaku, his close friend and classmate for another year, to catch up. From an outside standpoint, his eyes glared at Kitamura, as if saying, "I'll get that guy!" But, of course, that wasn't the case. He was just thinking calmly as he watched him approach.

There was no helping the misconceptions people might have about him. If another one happened, he'd just clear it up. After all, even if it took time to win them over, there were always some people like this guy who would figure it out eventually. He didn't like it, but...it was the only option, so what else could he do?

He looked up at the sky and squinted at its radiance. The day was beautiful, without even a breeze. The sakura petals fell without a sound, gently landing in Ryuuji's hair.

Still carrying all that stubborn, painful, mental baggage, he took another long step forward in the loafers he'd shined the night before.

It was wonderful weather for the opening ceremony.

"Yikes."

"I'm in the same class as Takasu-kun."

"He's as tough as they come."

"It's a little scary."

"Someone talk to him."

"No way, take it from me—that's impossible. You go."

"Hey, don't push me."

And so it went, on and on.

No matter what they say, Ryuuji thought, *I am the way I am. I won't be bothered by it.*

Ryuuji accepted the surrounding stares of his new classmates with indifference. Still seated at his desk, he turned his back slightly, causing people to avert their eyes. He quietly licked his parched lips. His jittering leg was an unconscious fidget. From the side, he looked like a predator, impatiently awaiting feeble prey. But that was just appearances.

"As always, it looks like a bunch of guys here totally have the wrong idea about you," Kitsamura said. "Well, that'll be fixed before long. I'm with you, and there's quite a few people from the original class A mixed in here, too."

"Yeah. It's fine, I don't mind it," Ryuuji replied with a thin smile.

The muttering from his classmates still hadn't let up. "I'm telling you," someone said. "He's in a good mood. Look at him— definitely licking his lips in cruel anticipation, stalking the prey in front of him."

In actuality, he felt like shooting out of his seat like a rocket, while grinning from ear to ear. And naturally, that feeling wasn't just from being in the same class as Kitamura. Something like that only warranted a smile and a, "We're together again, Kitamura."

The thing that made him so happy he wanted to jump for joy was—

"Hey, Kitamura-kun! We're in the same class this year!"

Because of her.

"Hm?" Kitamura said. "Huh, so you're in class C, too, Kushieda!"

"What, you only just noticed? You're so cold! It's a brand-new year; you could at least check the registry."

"Sorry, sorry. What a coincidence, though! I guess the meetings of student club presidents will be easier than ever."

"Ha ha, that's right! Oh, you were...Takasu-kun, right?" she asked, as she turned to Ryuuji. "I wonder if you remember me? We've had a few near misses, what with both of us hanging around Kitamura-kun."

Ryuuji said nothing.

"Uhhh? It's okay to call you Takasu-kun, right?" she said.

"...Ah, ye...kay." He fumbled for his words but was too taken aback by the sudden spectacle of a goddess assailing him. Her smile dazzled him, bursting out like the sun. It was as warm as the stolen light that once shined through his southern window, a warmth that suffused his vision all at once with radiant beams. The overflowing particles of light clung to him until Ryuuji could no longer keep his eyes open.

"Kushieda Minori, right?" he said.

Ah, if only, if only, if only! The sound of his own brusque voice made Ryuuji want to shout out loud. Why could he only answer like *that*, why couldn't he have said something more suave—

"Oh, hey! You remembered my whole name! Awesome—that sure makes me happy! Uhm, uh-oh, I think someone's trying to get my attention over there. Well then, Kitamura-kun. After school, we're having this year's first meeting for new second-years. Make sure you don't forget! See you later, too, Takasu-kun!"

Just about at his limits, Ryuuji tried raising a hand in courtesy...at her turned back. He was too late. She probably didn't even see.

But.

She said she was happy... She said she'd see me later...

Kushieda Minori had said that to him.

She said she was happy... She said she'd see me later...

Kushieda Minori, who he had *prayed* would be in his class, had said that.

She said she was happy... She said she'd see me later...

About me. About me!

She said she was happy!

"Takasu?"

"...Yeah?"

Suddenly Kitamura drew incredibly close, until Ryuuji bent away from him in his chair. "What are you grinning at?"

"Uh, n-nothing."

"I see." Kitamura pushed up his glasses with his center finger, and Ryuuji couldn't avoid feeling a certain admiration for Kitamura. The guy was probably the only person in the world who could detect one of Ryuuji's grins.

That wasn't the only thing Ryuuji admired him for, though.

"Kitamura," he said. "You're, like...really good at...talking to girls." (He meant Kushieda, of course.)

"Huh? What makes you say that?" Peering over his lenses, Kitamura's eyes showed no trace of humility—only genuine surprise. Somehow, he was completely unaware of his talent. Confronted with such a thick-skulled guy, Ryuuji held back his answer.

Kitamura's casual conversation with Kushieda Minori just a moment past had been more than successful—and it wasn't just that conversation, either. Ever since they were first-years, Kitamura was able to have pleasant conversations with Kushieda Minori, who was in the same softball club. Meanwhile, Ryuuji toiled endlessly, pitifully hard to earn leftover smiles and passing greetings. In soccer terms, he was the sweeper—though he'd never had a chance to play offense.

The reason Ryuuji started to think Kushieda Minori was cute, the reason that he liked her and wanted to become closer to her in the first place, was because he was constantly *right there*, getting to see how fun her conversations with Kitamura were.

It wasn't just that, though. It was because of her bright, ever-changing expressions. Her flexible body and exaggerated gestures. Her easygoing smile. Her unclouded voice.

Even though everyone else was afraid of him, from the start, she had been cheerfully broadminded and never deviated in that attitude toward Ryuuji.

He liked everything about Kushieda Minori. To him, all the elements that composed her seemed radiant, as though she were made from fragments of the sun. She was wholesome and straightforward—in his mind, she was nothing less than the perfect girl.

But even so.

"Don't be stupid. No *way* am I good at talking to girls. I bet you don't even know what all the girls call me, do you?"

Unconsciously, Ryuuji released a deep sigh. Despite how jealous he became while watching Kitamura's conversations—so jealous that he thought his eyes might bleed—his friend continued, unaware.

"I'm terrible with girls," he said. "I doubt I'll ever pull off dating one." *That* was his remark.

"I...don't think...that's the case," Ryuuji said. Looking up at such a dazzling gentleman, he again decided to swallow any other words he had. No matter how many times he said it, this guy definitely wouldn't understand. And that made Ryuuji feel miserable.

It was true that the girls called Kitamura "Maruo-kun." This was because he looked exactly like a certain character from a famous manga, an obnoxiously serious honor student. His intense glasses, straight-laced personality, outstanding grades, and frivolous fashion sense all put him distinctly apart from the norm. He was such a spitting image of Maruo that whenever he said the word "precisely"—the character's trademark phrase—the class would practically go into an uproar. On top of that, last year he'd also been the class president, and more recently had become the vice president of the student council. On top of that, he was also serving as the unofficial new president of the softball club. It was only fitting that he'd wind up as the subject of a joking comparison.

Still, he wasn't bad looking. No, in fact, if you looked closely, he was surprisingly handsome. Plus, he didn't have any two-faced qualities to his personality. He had a great sense of humor, and really, there just wasn't anything to dislike about him. And because of that, even though the girls targeted him for teasing, it wasn't mean-spirited.

Ah, that's right. Ryuuji understood. Whatever Kitamura might say, the girls did like him. It wasn't just Kushieda Minori. He could talk naturally to any girl. The girls would act like they were close and say, "Awww, I'm with Maruo again this year!" In response, he would make a light remark like, "What, you're unhappy about that?"

When you act like that, how can you say that you're bad with girls? You're not even hated like I am. Just as he was thinking this, he heard a voice say, "Y-yikes..."

There it was again.

When he overheard that word, he turned his gaze down and let the speaker go past. He felt like he could handle anything anybody might say about him. He was over the moon about being in the same class as Kushieda Minori; they'd never shared a class-room before.

But people kept talking.

"It's really amazing... You can tell just looking at him that he's not someone you should mess with."

"Yeah, those eyes are *intense*. Be careful—if he lost his temper, you'd be a goner."

And the spell was broken. Although the whispering voices probably harbored no ill will, the sheer number of them was start-ing to get to him. Until the new homeroom teacher came, hid-ing out in the restrooms might be the best thing for his peace of mind. With that thought in mind, he stood up. But the moment he headed for the hallway, something bumped lightly against his stomach.

"Oof...?"

It sure felt like he'd hit something, but he saw nothing in front of him. How strange. Ryuuji restlessly glanced around the vicinity. But what he saw was the faces of his classmates as they murmured all around him...

"Oh, man. Just as expected of Takasu-kun... He's made the first move."

"It's the ultimate showdown already... I knew this class would be trouble the moment I saw the registry."

They were probably going on about the look in his eyes.

"It's the battle that'll decide who's in charge...the clash of the delinquents!"

"It's like an amazing card just hit the table..."

They were acting strangely. *A battle? The delinquents? An amazing card? What are they talking about?* He turned his head to try and better grasp the situation—and then it happened.

"So, you run into someone, and you can't even apologize...?"

He heard a quiet voice from somewhere nearby. The speaker sounded strange, monotone, emotionally contained to an extreme degree—but it felt like they were just barely keeping the lid on an unparalleled explosion.

The voice's owner was nowhere to be seen.

"Uh...?"

Feeling a bit like he'd wandered into the Twilight Zone, Ryuuji slowly looked to his right. No one there. He looked to his left. No one there, either. Apprehensively, he looked in the scariest direction—up. *Good, no one there.*

"Which means..."

Sure enough, there she was. Way, way below his line of sight—far below even Ryuuji's chest—was the crown of someone's head.

His first impression of her was that of a doll. Any way you sliced it, she was small. Small, and enveloped in a long, cloud-like shroud of hair—it was the Palmtop Tiger.

"...The Palmtop Tiger?"

Without thinking, those enigmatic words suddenly popped into his mind and spilled right out of his mouth. He felt like he'd heard them from someone else, murmuring from far off.

The Palmtop Tiger. Is that her...?

"Who...?"

Is that supposed to describe the doll I see in front of me? Sure, palmtop works, but what makes this girl a tiger? On and on, his mind continued in this way.

"Who...exactly is supposed to be a 'Palmtop Tiger,' anyway?" Taiga asked.

It was no time to ponder the question. The "tiger" raised her chin slightly, then both her eyes.

"..........!"

Her stare lasted about three seconds. Ryuuji thought she had been scared stiff, but he was woefully mistaken.

A momentary vacuum had exploded like a bomb and had only just passed. Hearing was slow to return to Ryuuji's ears. When he came to, he was on his butt. It wasn't just Ryuuji. Several others had also collapsed close by, whimpering. Some were even trying to crawl away.

What just happened?

Then he understood.

Nothing had happened.

It was just—the girl in front of him.

"...You're irritating," she said.

All she had done was glare at Ryuuji with her two huge eyes. That was all. And yet, during those brief seconds of tension, Ryuuji had been simply overwhelmed. *Completely* overwhelmed. His mind had gone blank. Tension had immobilized his body, and he literally collapsed, right there.

He'd been so taken aback by her glowering stare—or more accurately, by the intensity it contained—that he had fallen right on his butt.

What had happened was way out there. It was on a completely different level. He had totally and completely lost. Ryuuji, who had never been bested when it came to his intimidating eyes, had lost by a country mile.

For the first time in his life, he understood. A truly savage gaze had a violent—no, murderous—weight to it.

"Hmph." After a few endless seconds of her gaze, which seemed to unwaveringly pierce right through his heart, she finally looked away, filled with contempt. "'Ryu,' is it? Like a dragon... How lame."

Her lips were like flower petals turned up by the wind. Her words struck like bullets and were just as child-like as she was.

She tousled her fluffy hair with an unbelievably small hand. Her eyes, their murderousness subdued, were now half-hidden by soft eyelids. They resembled the stare of a glass-eyed doll. Those transparent, hollow eyes reflected nothing at all as they gave Ryuuji a final once-over.

She was cute. She was terrifying.

Her milky white cheeks, her long, hazy ashen hair with its mysterious color, her delicate limbs and slender shoulders, the eyelashes that softened her gleaming eyes—she was cute as candy filled with lethal poison and as dainty as a flower bud with a deadly fragrance.

But, in the moment she glared at him, Ryuuji had seen a shape in her eyes. The form of a carnivore, bearing down on him. It was just an illusion, of course, but it had seemed more real than reality. Ryuuji had felt a weight of several tons pressing on him. His blood shuddered at the predator's roar; he felt it breathing down his neck. It seemed to say, *I can kill any of you any time I want.*

Its sharp claws and giant fangs had loomed close. The smell of blood and the beast had filled the room. The illusion, many times the size of the small girl, was none other than a tiger.

"Uh, uhhh...uh, uhm, uh... Yup yup yup yup..." Instinctively, Ryuuji nodded his head up and down. He clasped one hand against the other. *Right, of course. The Palmtop Tiger.* He didn't know who'd come up with that, but, "It fits perfectly, doesn't it..."

It had a certain flair. He admired whoever had coined the name.

Then he realized why she'd muttered *Ryu* along with her contemptuous gaze.

Either when he fell on his butt, or maybe while the illusory tiger tore him apart, his jacket zipper had opened. And so, his shirt was completely exposed—the shirt Yasuko had so enthusiastically bought him. The shirt with a gimmicky dragon on it, exactly the kind a delinquent would wear. It wasn't as though he'd worn that shirt, which sent totally the wrong message, because he wanted to. It was just convenient to use during laundry day, and he had figured no one would see it, anyway.

Intense embarrassment flashed over him as he quickly zipped his jacket. He was still slumped disgracefully on the floor, like a damsel just roughed up by hoodlums. Then someone briskly crossed in front of his gaze and said, "Taigaaa, you're late! You skipped out on the opening ceremony, didn't you?!"

"I woke up late. More importantly, I'm glad I'm in the same class as you again this year, Minorin."

"Yeah! I'm glad, too!"

It was Kushieda Minori herself.

Minori laughed as she touched the Palmtop Tiger's hair, as though they were close. She had endearingly called the tiger "Taigaaa," much like the Palmtop Tiger had called her "Minorin."

While Ryuuji watched, dumbfounded, he heard someone whisper. "In their first match, victory goes to Aisaka, the Palmtop Tiger."

"Now that you mention it, Takasu just looks scary. He doesn't really act like a delinquent at all."

"Huh? You think?"

"That's because he's no match for the Palmtop Tiger. At any rate, she's the real deal."

"Takasu-kun, are you okay? Aisaka lashing out at you on day one was really unfortunate."

It seemed that the misunderstandings were likely to be fixed faster than Ryuuji thought.

The Palmtop Tiger's outrageous, real name was Aisaka Taiga. She was one hundred and forty-five centimeters tall. She and Kushieda Minori were supposedly close friends.

If rumors held true, her prodigal father supposedly controlled the Japanese underworld, or was a genius karate master who controlled America's underworld—or something like that. She herself held an advanced karate belt but had been expelled after attacking her teacher—or something like that.

Supposedly, when they first started high school, one guy after another initially mistook her for a vain beauty and made insistent romantic advances. However, they all got brutally rejected—they were threatened, chewed out, torn up, and teased mercilessly. A whole mess of guys were now beyond any hope of recovery. It was said Aisaka left a path of male corpses in her wake.

Anyway, when it came to Aisaka Taiga, there was no end to the dark rumors. Whether those were myths or facts, what Ryuuji was sure about was that she ranked as the school's most dangerous creature.

Ryuuji learned all about those rumors over the days following the opening ceremonies.

2

EVEN WITH THE SHOCKING START, Takasu Ryuuji's high school life as a newly minted second-year student was going well.

There were several reasons for this.

For example, despite his most pessimistic expectations, the rumor that Takasu was a delinquent quickly evaporated. Along with Kitamura, he was lucky to have quite a few people from last year's class with him once again. But more than anything, the simple fact that he had been terrorized by the Palmtop Tiger on opening day sealed the deal: He was just a normal kid. (On that point and that point alone, he wanted to thank Aisaka Taiga.)

On top of all that, he also wasn't inconveniently pushed to join the student committee, and the seat he got by drawing straws was a window seat three rows from the front. It was in a location where he could pretty much lay back and relax. He also knew their homeroom teacher (Koigakubo Yuri, single with a capital "S," twenty-nine years old) from when she had been the assistant homeroom teacher the year before. Although she was getting on in years, and still single, she wasn't unhappy at all.

And then...

"...And then, the part near the rim of the bucket was solid, right? Like, the parts around the—what's it called? The parts around the *circumference* were solid. But then the entire center was still liquid, and if you tilted it, the jiggly parts around the circumference would go like this..."

"Ow!"

"Ah, Takasu-kun! Sorry!"

But the most important reason things were going well was this one:

The existence of his new classmate, Kushieda Minori. She was the sun that cast a beautiful, rose-colored tint over his life, his sunlight that shined without fail. That radiance would never harm him, but only warm his heart—even if, for example, it poked him in the eye.

"A-are you okay?! Sorry, I didn't know you were behind me! Ohh...I totally touched the squishy part, didn't I?"

"...Don't worry about it. It's not a big deal."

"I'm really sorry! ...Uh, what was I talking about? Oh yeah! Like I was saying before, the part around the rim of the bucket that firmed up, right, was like this..."

"Ow!"

"Yikes! I think I got you even *deeper* that time. Sorry!"

Despite that incident, which he magnanimously waved away, Ryuuji was happy. As Minori bowed her head down in apology, an indescribable floral fragrance wafted from her hair. Regardless of what had happened, as she apologized, her eyes were currently looking at him, and only him. Getting poked in the eye twice was nothing compared to that happiness.

It didn't even matter whether she was talking to him or not. It would have been enough if she were just talking to someone near his seat. He could listen to Minori's voice forever, sweet enough you could practically smell it, and when she swung her arm around to describe the circumference of that bucket, her fingertip even touched him—touched his eyeball, to be exact, but still: She had touched him!

But why were *they talking about a bucket just now?* His face must have looked puzzled, because she explained: "I, like, made pudding...in a bucket."

"Don't hurt anybody else," Minori said, admonishing her own finger as she grabbed it with her other hand. Then she gave Ryuuji a very thorough explanation. *No, wait*—what she actually said was, "Takasu-kun, do you like pudding?"

They were having a conversation. Ryuuji's heart suddenly skipped a beat. He couldn't respond with anything sensible. He was well and truly flummoxed. Even mustering the full strength of his will, all he could say was, "Yeah..."

She probably thought he was a boring guy. She probably

didn't want to talk to him anymore. But Minori was already leaving Ryuuji behind, unaware of the inner turmoil that never reached his face. Minori's charming cheeks took on a rosy color as she continued. "Bucket. Pudding. A woman's greatest weakness."

"But I just couldn't get it right! Getting it to firm up is hard. Still, because it's so big, the gooey parts and jiggly bits live in perfect harmony... Oh, I know—Takasu-kun, do you want to judge it for yourself? As an apology for poking you in the eye."

"Wha? J-judge it...?"

She couldn't mean she wanted him to try a taste of her home-made pudding, could she? Did she really mean that she wanted *him* to try it? Ryuuji's gaze intensified as he looked at Minori's adorable, smiling face.

Minori nodded. "Yeah! I'll bring it over right now, so you can take a look at it."

If this kind of happiness waited on the other side, what a lucky day, to be poked in the eye! However, as Minori cheerfully made her way to her own seat, and Ryuuji's eyes bored into her back, he felt a sudden urge to flee.

Once he received the pudding, what expression was he supposed to make as he ate it? And wouldn't it be weird for a guy like him to be slurping up pudding when it wasn't even lunch time? And before he even considered all of *that*, was it the type of thing he was supposed to eat straight away, or was he supposed to thank her for it and put in his bag?

"I-I don't... I don't know..."

He stroked his cheek nervously, but for the time being, he cleaned the notebooks off his desk, just in case he got his heart set on eating it right there.

Both nervous and excited, Ryuuji skillfully averted his gaze as Minori came back. She was so bright he couldn't look at her. Minori tilted her head and stopped right in front of Ryuuji with a brilliant smile on her face. Then she said, "Here, Takasu-kun. Here you go."

Her voice was so gentle, he could hear a heart emoji follow his name. Ryuuji nervously lifted his face and, with both hands, reverently received the pudding.

"O-oh. How nice..."

It was thinner than he thought it would be—lighter, too...

"...That you took these pictures..."

"But it's kind of gross, right?"

When she said, *judge it for yourself*, she had meant to judge the pictures—not the flavor. And on top of that, the thing in the photo looked downright disgusting. His brain felt like a crashed web browser. A huge bucket lay squarely planted on a vinyl rug, and inside it was a dead squid, pale yellow in color... No, worse— it was filled with something that looked like slime. He felt like he was letting Minori down, but no matter how he looked at it, it just didn't look like pudding. In the second photo, the part-liquid, part-solid slime had dribbled onto the vinyl.

"It tasted weird, too," she said, as he looked at the third picture. "Maybe I didn't wash the bucket well enough?"

In the picture Ryuuji now had in hand, Minori was sitting down with one knee bent, eating the slime with a massive spoon. *I'll take just this one,* Ryuuji thought for a fleeting moment, but then she spoke again, interrupting the thought.

"Thanks for looking at them! I've got to show them to Taiga, too. Huh? Where did she go? Wasn't she just over there a second ago?"

Minori quickly collected her photos. Then she darted away from Ryuuji to search for her companion, the Palmtop Tiger Aisaka Taiga, who had vanished unnoticed. And with that, the time had run out on his dream.

Taiga, too, huh?

Ryuuji involuntarily let out a sigh as he watched the apple of his eye disappear into the hallway in search of her friend.

It was an unexpected blessing that Minori was in the same class. Every day, be it during class or whenever, he got to see Minori. He could see her smile without having to peek from into some class he wasn't part of. To return to soccer terms, sometimes even being a steady sweeper paid off. If this wasn't happiness, what was?

Still, if he wanted to get even closer to Minori, there was one huge problem he had to overcome. That problem was that more often than not, she hung out with Aisaka Taiga.

Other than the incident during opening ceremonies, Ryuuji had tried to avoid getting involved with Aisaka, who somehow seemed to be an *actual* thug. Avoiding her, however, inevitably created a new problem: He couldn't approach Minori. (Granted, there were plenty of other reasons why he couldn't start up a conversation with her.)

He was about as interesting to Aisaka as the husk of a dead bug. As long as Ryuuji kept his distance, they didn't really make any contact, and it seemed unlikely that any real harm would come his way. Ryuuji's current goal was to do his best to avoid getting involved with the Palmtop Tiger and get close to Minori alone. If he could just accumulate more lucky moments like the bucket incident and turn them to his advantage, it might not be completely impossible.

All things considered, Ryuuji's bittersweet days were going pretty well.

...At least until school ended that day.

"Uh..."

When Ryuuji opened the door, he stood stock-still, at a loss for words. There were two chairs—no wait, three—flying through the air.

As they smashed onto the floor, he saw a single shadow in the middle of all the racket. It flitted across the edge of his vision, kicking at the chairs.

What on earth is going on? As Ryuuji narrowed his eyes into a dreadful glare, he was so bewildered by the truth that his breath stopped. He'd been asked to do some odd jobs after finishing the day's chores, so it was long after the end of school—no one should have been in the classroom. But he'd seen her.

He was certain he saw a uniformed girl jump headfirst behind a locker to hide, at the very moment she caught sight of Ryuuji. He definitely saw her, right at that moment, and he had certainly heard the loud noise she made when she kicked at the chairs. On top of that, he could still see her. There was a full-length mirror set up on the classroom wall and her back and head were reflected there, facing away.

The little klutz had curled up into an incredibly tiny, compact ball—cowering. Completely unaware of the mirror, she was stretching her neck out and peeking stealthily out at Ryuuji.

Ryuuji swallowed and decided to pretend he hadn't noticed— for that tiny, suspicious klutz's identity was none other than...the Palmtop Tiger. The reflection of her back in the mirror gave him more than enough information to know for sure. Part of it was that long hair and the white profile of her face, but most of all it was because, out of everyone he knew, Aisaka was the only one who could make herself that tiny. *But why her, out of all people?* he wondered.

I saw nothing. I know nothing. I noticed nothing.

Taking that mantra to heart, Ryuuji proceeded into the room. He really didn't want to go into the classroom, where the Palmtop Tiger lurked for reasons unknown, but he had left his bag on his desk, and he couldn't just go home without it.

The classroom was silent in the twilight, as though he had crossed the threshold into some spider's trap, a web spun by Aisaka. The moment he set foot in the room, it felt like his soul was being ripped from his body. Cautiously, gingerly, Ryuuji did his best to feign a casual air as he moved his feet. In order to avoid provoking Aisaka, he tried to play oblivious, but then...

"AAHHH!"

Ridiculously, a faint cry of urgent despair echoed throughout the classroom.

Something came rolling out that completely undid all of Ryuuji's efforts. Aisaka Taiga, until then curled up, lost her balance. She flopped out from behind the locker with a forward somersault and, in a stroke of bad luck, landed right in front of Ryuuji.

"..."

"..."

Aisaka looked up. Ryuuji looked down. Neither of them had the luxury of ignoring each other anymore. Their gazes crossed, and they remained silent. They stayed like that for several seconds.

"A-are you okay?"

At long last, Ryuuji finally managed to choke out some words. Then, he extended a tentative hand out towards Aisaka, while she slowly got up. In response, she gave him a nearly inaudible reply.

"No thanks," she said, or "I don't know"—or something along those lines. From between the strands of her disheveled hair, Aisaka's steely eyes effortlessly cleaved straight through Ryuuji.

Instinctively, he took a large step back. Noticing the opening, Aisaka shakily came to a standing position. Head still hidden, she dusted off her skirt and took long strides to distance
herself from Ryuuji. She put her back to the window and narrowed her eyes, but didn't make any moves to leave the classroom. *Isn't she embarrassed?* A normal person would have been,
but it seemed those kinds of thoughts weren't of any concern to
the Palmtop Tiger.

If Aisaka was going to stay, then naturally, Ryuuji would have
to leave first.

"M-my bag," he muttered purposefully, before darting towards it.

Aisaka Taiga still stood by the window, watching him word-
lessly. He didn't know what sort of expression was on her face,
because he couldn't even bear to look at her. He just tried his best
to dampen the sound of his footsteps and make himself invisible
as he crossed the classroom. He could feel goosebumps prickling
across his cheek, where he sensed her glare, but he couldn't show
her a reaction. He couldn't provoke her. If he could get through
this without anything happening...

The bag wasn't at his desk—instead, it was where he'd left it
on top of Kitamura's, where they had been talking earlier. If he
could just get that bag, he could withdraw from the classroom.
Controlling his impatience, he stretched out his arm. Just twenty
centimeters away, ten centimeters away...

"Ah!" she said, jumping up.

He must have done something wrong. He *must* have done something wrong, to make Aisaka Taiga yell out at him. Ryuuji looked over his shoulder in dread and stared at the small doll standing by the window. "Wh-what...?"

"J-just what...d-do you think you're doing?" she asked.

Spontaneously, an eye-catching scene began to unfold right there on the spot. The Palmtop Tiger was reeling.

"I just came to get my bag," he said. "But...A-Aisaka? What's wrong? You're acting pretty weird."

Her puckered mouth opened and closed, and she shuffled her feet, as though performing some odd dance. As she brought a wavering finger up to her cheek, she started to jitter and shake. "Uhhhh, you mean, that's *your* bag? But that's not your chair. Wh-wh-wh-why, h-h-h-h-how?" she stammered, as she admonished Ryuuji.

"...I didn't mean anything by it," he said. "A teacher just called me while I was talking to Kitamura...and I just left it here... Argh!"

Aisaka, standing totally flummoxed several meters away from him, closed the gap in moments. *Where does she hide all that athleticism in such a tiny body?*

"Urk...! Urgh...ugh!" She pulled at the bag Ryuuji clutched to his chest, trying to rip it away. She wrenched at it with incredible strength.

"Whoa, whoa, whoa?! A-Aisaka?!"

"G-give! It! Back! Hand it over!"

From up close, he could see her cheeks turn a red that rivaled the sunset. Her cute face distorted into a bloodcurdling, demonic mask.

"Give it back, *give it,* I'm telling you!"

"Uggh!" He wouldn't let go. Out of pure, stubborn machismo, Ryuuji planted his feet solidly on the ground. Besides, if he were to release his grip now, Aisaka's tiny body would go flying.

To think he put all that effort into reading the situation for nothing.

"Hnnnngh!" She twisted her hips, dug her nails into the bag, and squeezed her eyes shut as her face went red, until a blood vessel popped out on her temple. She was determined to win their contest of strength.

Little by little, Ryuuji's fingers were slipping. Even his braced legs were slowly edging forward. Simply put, he'd probably lose. He couldn't bear it any longer.

"W-watch o...! Caref—stooop...!" he said.

"Hnnnnnnnnnnnnngh! Ah? Aaah!"

I can't do it anymore! he thought, but in that moment, Aisaka suddenly threw her head back. He saw a distant look in her eyes as her little hands flung wide open, and she let go... *SHE LET GO?!*

"ARGH!"

"ACHOO!"

CRASH!

The scream was Ryuuji. The sneeze, Aisaka. The crash was also Ryuuji. Scream, sneeze, the back of his head.

CHAPTER 2

When Aisaka's sneeze loosened her grip, Ryuuji had naturally flown backwards. He stumbled, bag still grasped in both hands, and slammed his head into the teacher's desk.

"Ow, oww... Th-that hurt! Wh-why...y-you...that *really* freakin' hurt! Were you trying to kill me or something?!" He was half crying as he protested.

"Ugh." Even after sending Ryuuji flying with her peculiar sneeze, Aisaka seemed oblivious of her surroundings. She sniffled, wobbled over to a desk, and hunched down.

"A-Aisaka? Hey, what's wrong?"

She curled up into a ball, her long hair draping all the way to the floor. She made a low moan but didn't answer. Was she feeling sick? He rubbed the back of his head and rushed over. He peeked at her face, which had just been bright red, but was now rapidly losing color. Her quivering lips were white as paper. Her forehead had strangely broken out into a sweat.

"Whoa... You're white as a sheet. Are you anemic? Here, grab my hand."

She had the same symptoms as Yasuko when she had collapsed, once. This time, he didn't hesitate to offer his hand.

"Tsk!" Aisaka vigorously brushed his hand away with her ice-cold fingers. She was still wobbling heavily, but—steadying herself with a nearby desk—she stood up.

"A-Aisaka! Are you okay?" he said.

Of course, she didn't answer. She started walking, knocking into desks along the way, as her velvety hair fluttered. He watched her diminutive back as she ran off. Because she had been sitting, the seat of her pleated skirt was folded up, and though it revealed a risqué amount of her delicate legs, she made her escape too fast for him to tell her.

"Wait up! Shouldn't you at least go to the nurse's office to rest?"

Even though he might have been meddling, Ryuuji couldn't just leave her, so he started to follow.

"Get away from me, you moron!" She shrieked, her desperate voice hitting him like a physical blow. He put on the brakes. If she could yell like that, she was probably fine...

"M-man, what a mess..."

The sound of Aisaka's running feet faded down the hallway until he stood alone in the classroom, still reeling in the aftermath of being called a moron.

Abandoned, Ryuuji just stood there, muttering weakly to himself.

The back of his head was still pounding, and Aisaka's nails had left ten lacerations in the side of the bag—the one they had failed to reach any sort of civil compromise on. The once neat rows of desks were unbearably jostled.

It was a mess.

The desks and Aisaka were both messed up. What a troublesome girl.

As he fussed with the desks until they were back in order, Ryuuji desperately tried to make sense of what had just happened. The after-school classroom that should have been deserted, Aisaka

Taiga somersaulting out, the bag that had nearly been stolen from him, the sneeze, the bump to the back of his head, the anemic girl... It was impossible, there was no understanding it. He didn't have a clue what to make of it.

"I'm no good with messed-up situations like these," Ryuuji solemnly mumbled to himself and sighed.

Little did he know, but the meaning of the incident was to become all too clear three hours later.

To: Kitamura Yuusaku-sama.
From: Aisaka Taiga.
"Th-this...is..."

It was seven at night. Yasuko had left early to accompany a customer to her job, so Ryuuji was eating a simple dinner alone. Finally, he had come to understand the meaning of the mysterious and now vaguely-remembered incident that happened earlier that day after school.

When he had gone back to his four-and-a-half tatami room to finish his homework, he opened his bag to take out his textbook and notebook—and that was when he had found it.

A light pink envelope. Pieces of silver foil were incorporated into the pulpy paper, shaped like cherry blossom petals. They seemed to flutter as they scattered through the paper, creating a texture like that of washi paper.

To Kitamura Yuusaku-sama, it was addressed.

He flipped it over. *From Aisaka Taiga*, it said. *To put this very politely, if this letter causes you trouble, please just throw it away.*

It was written in the faint blue ink of a nearly depleted pen.

No matter how he looked at it, this wasn't just a regular letter. It wasn't the class newsletter, and it didn't seem like a money envelope for repayment, either.

"This is...a love letter...!"

He was shocked. He had stumbled into something terrible.

Letting curiosity get the best of him was unthinkable, but his eyes narrowed mercilessly as he looked at the envelope. Of course, he wasn't angry—just extremely flustered.

Long story short, it seemed the Palmtop Tiger had gotten the wrong bag. She had mistaken his bag for Kitamura's and snuck this thing inside. That was why she had become so desperate and tried to steal it back.

"You put this in accidentally, didn't you?" he said aloud, trying to practice what he might say to her, acting as though nothing was up. "I didn't look inside, so I can't imagine what's in it. Ahhh well—here, you can have it back..." He shook his head. "Nope. That won't work."

He instantly snapped back to reality. That definitely wouldn't work. This was terrible. There was no way anyone would be fooled with a line like that. But he couldn't think of anything better. The next day, he'd have to hand the thing over to Aisaka quickly and casually with that line.

This is definitely a love letter, but I myself don't think it's a love letter. So, don't go thinking that I know a secret about you, or anything inconvenient like that, he'd say. Pretty far-fetched, but he'd try something along those lines. There was no other way. That was the one and only way to do it that wouldn't cause Aisaka embarrassment, and that wouldn't hurt his own pride or cause him any distress.

Ryuuji forced himself to believe it and started to put that dangerous thing back into his bag. That was when it happened.

"Eeeep..."

His heart constricted and jumped.

The envelope, held so carefully in the palm of his hand to keep from getting it dirty or damaged, started to unseal itself right before his eyes. *Stop it, don't open!* he shouted a silent prayer. But it seemed that part of the already weak adhesive had bent itself out of shape and was peeling off.

He forgot everything but how to breathe. Soon, the envelope opened completely, there in Ryuuji's hand.

Just like that, a letter-snooping miscreant was born.

"N-no... No, you've got it all wrong, I didn't see anything! That's right, I'll reseal it! If I do that, she won't find out!"

"That's right!" Inko-chan gave him a shout of encouragement from the living room, as Ryuuji ransacked his drawers looking for glue. He finally found some and was all set to restore the envelope. He wouldn't leave any evidence behind, but...

"...H-huh?"

In spite of himself, his busy hands stopped.

The envelope had nothing in it. With some hesitation, he opened the envelope again, peeked inside, and held it to the light for confirmation. There really was nothing in it. It was empty.

What a relief.

Feeling spent, Ryuuji involuntarily slumped across his desk. *Don't just scare someone like that—what a klutz.*

Aisaka Taiga. You're *the one who's a moron.*

Hiding in a completely obvious place, somersaulting out into the open, getting the wrong bag, sneezing and falling down while trying to steal it, and—on top of all that—forgetting to put the letter into the envelope. Even for a klutz, that was just too much.

Even after pulling himself together, Ryuuji didn't have the heart to continue the idiotic operation of regluing an empty envelope.

The next day, when he returned it to Aisaka, could he really pretend to be indifferent? It might be fine, as long as he didn't burst out in laughter over the ridiculous details of this story, but in the unlikely event that he did do something like that, this might be the time he really did get eaten by the Palmtop Tiger.

Nevertheless, he decided to finish regluing the envelope.

The strange night wore on—until two in the morning.

Ryuuji suddenly woke up. He opened his eyes wide in a daze.

He felt as though he'd been having a dream, but...the clock indicated it was the dead of night. He scratched vigorously at his belly. He always slept like a baby until morning—why had he woken up at such an odd time? Ryuuji hadn't the faintest idea.

It may have been because he slept with just a t-shirt and his underwear, but he felt a bit chilly. It was the middle of April, but apparently, he had fallen asleep with the window open. Nothing lay beyond the window but the wall of that upper-class condominium—so lately, his vigilance had waned. There wasn't anything around worth stealing, but he reached out his arm and closed the window anyway, making sure to properly lock it.

He got up from his bed, an old mail-order purchase. Still feeling unsettled, he stifled a lethargic yawn. Maybe a bad dream was to blame, but his heart was pounding. The atmosphere felt inexplicably strange, almost as if he were being watched.

"I have a bad feeling..." he muttered. Wobbly, he stepped onto the tatami mats and checked his phone to make sure nothing had happened to Yasuko. But there was nothing there to speak of, not even a text from the bar. He took a breath. *I guess it was nothing.*

Since he was already up, he headed barefoot to the restroom, and then on toward the cold wooden floor of the kitchen.

But in that instant...

"Huhh?!"

He felt a tingle run down his neck. Reflexively, he turned around—and completely slipped on a discarded newspaper, falling down butt-first. BAM! Butt, meet floor. The impact ran from his waist to his head, all the air momentarily knocked out of him.

"...!"

He couldn't even get out a scream.

With tremendous force, something careened down through the air, right where Ryuuji's head had just been. After a powerful swing and miss, it struck the floor with a foreboding clamor, just beside Ryuuji's body.

"Tsk...tsk...tsk."

An ominous human silhouette hovered in the pitch-black, two-bedroom apartment. It took aim at Ryuuji, once again swinging that rod-shaped object at him in a wide arc. He was under attack.

He didn't understand why, though. He wanted it to be a dream. *Someone help!*

Still unable to make a sound, Ryuuji desperately rolled away for dear life. He needed light, or the police, or the landlady. His mind went blank. He couldn't think. Scared stiff, he could do nothing but run away, nothing but crawl to the front entrance. But...

"HIYAHHHHH!"

Now he was done for. His assailant pointed the murder weapon at the top of his head and then struck. Without even knowing what was happening, in the spur of the moment, he reached out with both hands and...

"Ah...? I-I did it...!"

Somehow, he stopped the blow precisely with his bare hands. Well, he probably hadn't been precise about it, but through sheer luck, he had the murder weapon firmly grasped between his palms.

"Ugh!"

The perpetrator pushed that weapon forcefully downwards. Ryuuji used all his strength to try and force it back. As they waged their silent test of strength, the figure wavered in the darkness. A small stature, an outline engulfed in long hair—*of course*, he thought, somewhere in the back of his mind. He had probably suspected who it was from the very beginning.

Gritting his teeth, toughing through it, Ryuuji came to a strange understanding. Of course—of *course*—who else would do something this messed up?

But at the very moment he figured out who the perpetrator was—*Aah! I can't do it anymore!*—both of his shaking hands lost all sensation. The stiff muscles in the back of his neck also strained to their limits.

"...Hah... Ahhh..."

HACHOO!

His opponent lost balance for an instant.

At the moment of that strange-sounding sneeze, the weight on him suddenly, softly disappeared. His opponent succumbed to Ryuuji's strength, and he pushed back, staggering wildly.

"Ah! Wah!" his opponent quietly exclaimed, then tottered, tripped, and landed on the bed with a resounding thump. Ryuuji stood up and slammed into the wall, rushing to turn on the light switch.

"AISAKAAAAA!"

"..."

"You could at least use a tissue!"

He threw a tissue box at the Palmtop Tiger, Aisaka Taiga, who was nonchalantly wiping her nose on the bedspread.

Her long, fluffy hair spilled down her back, and she wore a dress covered in layers of lace and other fluffy materials. Considering her tiny body, styles that added volume to her frame really suited her...

"H-hand over the wooden sword." Ryuuji found himself deeply regretting that he hadn't managed to steal away Aisaka Taiga's weapon.

Since he'd turned on the light and given her the tissues, nothing about the perilous situation had been settled at all. Both Aisaka's eyes glinted with light. She circled the small room's edge, just like a tiger cornering its prey in a cage. Naturally, Ryuuji kept his distance. Still in his underwear, he too ran in circles around the room, trying to keep away from her.

But no matter how long they kept doing that, they wouldn't get anywhere. That thought in mind, he said, "Hey, Aisaka... I know what you want. You want me to give back that lo—that letter, right? The one you accidentally put in my bag."

"...Tsk."

He'd summoned the courage to speak. But at that very moment, Aisaka swallowed her breath and went still. From his perspective, her whole body seemed to grow. She was a bomb about to go off. Her fuse had been lit.

"I-I'll give it back! So calm down! I didn't look inside!"

"...It's not enough to just give it back," she answered, voice so low that it seemed to creep along the ground. "That's nowhere near good enough... You shouldn't even know that the letter exists." She whisked the gigantic wooden sword up, so that it danced elegantly above her head.

"DIE!"

"GAH!"

She aimed straight for the top of Ryuuji's head and brought the sword down.

Just how fast is *this girl?!*

Aisaka leaped at Ryuuji's chest, crossing several meters in an instant. If her sword hadn't hit the wall (the security deposit!), he really would have been done for.

"Tsk!"

"You idiot!" On the verge of tears, he leaped back and let loose a heartfelt shout. "Are you out of your mind?! What kind of nutcase would try to kill her own classmate? You're messed up!"

"Shut up! Now that you know about the letter, I can't bear to live with the shame! The only thing left for me to do—is *die*!" The sword's point lunged for his Adam's apple.

"Yikes! Y-you say *you'll* die, so why are you trying to kill *me*?!"

Ryuuji avoided it with downright miraculous reflexes, but Aisaka's power was immense. She used that power to cut straight into the sliding door (the repair bill!), then followed through

with another lunge. In those wide-open eyes, there was no hesitation, just desperation and resolve.

"I'd rather kill you than kill myself! Sorry, but please die! And if you can't manage that—erase all your memories!"

"How the heck am I supposed to do that?!"

"Trust me, it's not impossible! If I..." She glanced at the wooden sword she brandished. "If I knock you over the head with this, even if you survive, it should at least give you amnesia."

"No knocking, thanks!"

Just how stubborn was she?! If only he could get her to realize she was talking nonsense. But words wouldn't get through to her. Common sense, common courtesy, morality—stuff like that didn't matter to Aisaka.

Ugh, that's why I didn't want to get involved with her in the first place!

Contrary to Ryuuji's thoughts, which were turning grim, Aisaka's destructive conduct was going splendidly. If Ryuuji kept on running, she'd just corner him. She knocked the boxes off the top of the wardrobe, ripped a hole in the sliding door, and kicked over a small table. While it fell, she exclaimed: "Forget about the love letter!"

The Palmtop Tiger was self-destructing. He could have said he didn't know it was a love letter (that had been an option), but now she'd confirmed it herself, making things a real mess. No, that wasn't right—things had been a mess since the very first moment he got involved with Aisaka. And on top of that...

"You looked at it, right?!" she said. "You read it, didn't you?! And then you thought I was an idiot, an id... an id... Uhh, uguh, uwuhhh...!"

"Ah?! Wait—a-are you crying?"

"No way!"

Between those horrible, groaning noises, she released a half-suppressed sigh. She aimed her wide eyes at Ryuuji, their whites turned faintly red. Tears welled up at their corners. Even though it was only a tiny bit, Aisaka really was crying. *He* was the person that ought to cry! If he thought he could afford to collapse right then and there, he would have, but at that moment, it would mean his life.

Ugh, what a weird turn of events. He was the one being attacked, so why did he feel like he was the one who had done something wrong?

Then, out of complete desperation, he feinted a run to the side and made a risky grab for Aisaka's wrist. She was shocked for one brief moment. He felt a little scared that her delicate wrist might break in his grasp.

"Let go!"

Whatever she said, he needed to play his trump card now. He inhaled, preparing to shout with all his might. *Sorry, neighbors. Landlady, please forgive me.*

"No way am I letting go!" he barked. "Now listen here! Aisaka, you made a terrible mistake! That envelope was—"

"Let! Go! Of! Me!"

Aisaka's struggling wrist slipped from Ryuuji's hand. She tried aiming at him from close range. Her bloodthirsty eyes glistened.

"It was empty!"

Ryuuji got his words out just in time. The wooden sword's swing stopped at the very last moment, directly above his head, lightly brushing several strands of his hair.

Several all-too-unpleasant seconds of silence went by. Finally, she squeezed out a word. "Emp...ty...?" she said in that immature voice of hers. He nodded his head fervently up and down.

"Th-that's right. It was empty. So, I haven't seen whatever was meant to be inside and also, that's right—that's right! You were lucky you didn't give that to Kitamura! You avoided making a fool out of yourself in front of everybody."

Bleary eyes still wide open, Aisaka froze in place. Ryuuji took the opportunity to crawl away. He grabbed his bag and rummaged through it with shaking hands. In a mad rush, he pulled out the envelope.

"See! See, see!"

He pushed the envelope into her small hands as her eyes became bloodshot. The wooden sword dropped to the floor with a thud, Aisaka's body trembling violently. But she stood firm, righted herself, and raised the newly returned envelope up to the light.

"...Oh..."

Her mouth puckered, half-open.

"O-oh...ooh...ohhh! Whaa!"

Messing up her tangled hair, Aisaka cut open the envelope's seal. As if going mad, she shook it upside down to confirm it was empty, then looked back at Ryuuji in blank amazement.

"...You klutz."

At his leaden proclamation, she sat down unsteadily right where she was standing. Her eyes opened so wide they seemed like they might tear at the corners. Before long, they developed a faint film. Her thin, open lips quivered and shook, and she seemed to be trying to say something, but she could only bob her chin.

"A-Aisaka?"

Her brain had crashed.

Before Ryuuji's eyes, her face suddenly turned pale white. Then, right there in the living room of his shabby two-bedroom apartment, her petite frame, padded by the oversized dress, toppled over.

"Hey! Aisaka! Are you okay?!"

At that surprising turn of events, Ryuuji rushed over and held her unconscious, doll-like body—and that was when it happened.

GRRRROOOOOOOWWWWWWWWLLLL.

"...I-Is that your *stomach*...?"

The Takasu household always had frozen food.

They had never run out of garlic or ginger, and always had a stock of onions. He also had leftover turnip stalk and leaves, and some bacon he had been thinking of using for breakfast. Eggs, too.

Of course, it was rare that they would do something so foolish as run out of seasonings. Naturally, they also had instant consommé (for when he needed to cut corners), Ajinomoto seasoning, and chicken bone soup stock available in the kitchen.

He got a heaping bowl of rice, seasoned it with sesame oil, and chopped up the turnip stalks. He added egg and the rice was soon wrapped in a golden sheen. He could leave the rest to the green onion's flavor and the umami of the bacon. He added Ajinomoto to taste, pinches of salt and pepper, a subtle amount of oyster sauce, and, as a finishing touch, scattered chives on the stock.

Simply adding hot water and shards of onion, he garnished the chicken bone soup in just under fifteen minutes. He finished washing the dishes in the process.

Even though it was three in the morning on a weekday, Ryuuji's skills didn't falter.

Guuuuurrrrgllle. And then, over the almost comical sound of her stomach, he heard a faint, incoherent mumbling interposed. "G-garlic..."

He was hesitant to touch her, so he said, "...Aisaka. Aisaka Taiga, wake up. Your wish for garlic is fulfilled, and it's infused with the aroma of sesame oil, no less."

The petite body he had laid out on the bed jolted. "Fry... fry..."

"That's right. It's fried rice."

"Fried...rice..."

He saw drool dripping from her pale lips...and because he saw it, he had to wipe it away. He carefully dabbed at her mouth with a tissue.

"Here, wake up. It'll get cold."

Aisaka's eyelashes fluttered faintly. In order to avoid touching her body directly, he grabbed her by her clothes and lifted her from the sheets. In the middle of that, Aisaka wriggled in apparent displeasure.

"Ah...wha?"

It seemed she'd finally woken up. She gave an irritated scowl, brushing off Ryuuji's arm. With visible distrust, she peeled off the damp towel he'd put on her forehead. But then her nostrils flared. "...Huh? What's that? It smells like garlic..." She looked curiously around the room.

"I just said it was fried rice. Hurry up and eat. You need to get your blood sugar up or you'll keel over again."

When he pointed at the table setting he'd prepared with the fried rice, her eyes glittered for a moment, but then she said, "What's your deal?"

Her eyes narrowed, and she glared at Ryuuji in his tracksuit with a taciturn look.

"There isn't any *deal*. If someone collapses right in front of you, fried rice is the only answer. It was ridiculous—the sound your stomach made. I can only imagine what it'd be like if you got anemic at school and...hey, you haven't been eating *anything*, have you?"

"Leave me alone, it's none of your business. Do you live alone here?"

"Sometimes my mom's home. Right now, she's at work. If you're going to invade somebody's household, at least get a sense of it, first. Any other place would've called the cops on you by now."

"Shut up. You're not up to anything weird, are you?"

Aisaka was still pale, but she purposefully guarded her body with both hands. She gave Ryuuji a scrutinizing look, challenging him with her glare. He wanted to yell out, *You're way weirder than me!* But instead he said, "Someone who just came off an attempted home invasion and then collapsed from hunger doesn't get the right to complain. Just eat."

At any rate, it was three in the morning. He couldn't let her disturb the peace any more than she already had.

"Listen h—ubgh!"

He took a heaping spoonful of fried rice and forced it into Aisaka's mouth, right where she lay, complaining on the bed. It took a considerable amount of courage, but Ryuuji was already in despair, so what did he have to lose? He overflowed with a spirit of gallantry.

"Whaareouing!"

Glaring, Aisaka pushed away the spoon. But—probably because she couldn't spit out what was already in her mouth—she chewed, her small cheeks puffed out like a squirrel.

"Y—*gulp!* You—don't think you'll be able to just get away with this..." *Gulp.* She swallowed. "Don't even think our conversation is over yet."

She stole the spoon from Ryuuji's hand—the same spoon she had just pushed away. "First of all, I've figured out why the envelope was empty." She hopped off the bed, dragging along her trailing skirt. "You tried looking at it and unsealed it. You're the lowest of the low. A Peeping Tom." She turned her back to Ryuuji as she sat down at the table.

"You've got it all wrong. How do I say this... I only noticed because it was see-through." It was a lie, but oh well. He couldn't tell whether she was listening or not. Aisaka, still seated, took a small spoonful from the mountain of fried rice and quietly brought it to her small mouth, oddly tense.

She chewed, chewed, and swallowed. She touched her mouth to the spoon, too. For a moment, her expression was one of relish, and then she took another bite. Ryuuji sat across from Aisaka and started to put words to what he'd pondered while making the fried rice.

"Now that you mention it, Aisaka, listen to what I have to say for a second. In the first place..."

Nom nom nom nom.

"...You said you were embarrassed that I saw that letter... Or actually, the envelope or whatever, right?"

Nom nom nom nom nom nom nom nom... Cough! "Gah!"

"What I think is..." he tried to say.

Munch munch munch munch munch munch munch munch munch munch munch munch munch munch munch munch munch!

"Listen to me!"

"Seconds!"

"Fine!"

Good thing I made a lot, Ryuuji muttered silently, as he placed the entire contents of the fry pan on her plate. He served it to Aisaka.

"Now listen to what I have to say!"

No matter how much he shouted, it was useless. It was like talking to a wall. This was what they meant by "having blinders on." He wondered where she packed all that food away in such a tiny body, while Aisaka focused solely on the fried rice. Fried rice fried rice fried rice fried rice... It was a one-woman fried rice feast.

He wouldn't get anywhere with her like this. The very words "fried rice" were losing their meaning to him. Ryuuji quietly made a decision. He brought a lethal weapon out from the corner of the living room, hidden by a cloth.

"Hey, Aisaka—look at this. I'll show you something juicy."

"Something juicy?!"

When she reacted with a lift of her head—*BAM*—he took off the cloth and showed it to her.

"GAH!"

"What do you think? It's gross, right?"

Able to sleep through a level four earthquake, it was the positively disgusting, sleeping face of Takasu's Inko-chan. Spasming, the whites of her eyes showing, her mouth half open, her weird tongue lolling out—it had immediate results. Aisaka leaped backwards.

"It's *way* gross! Why would you show me something like that?"

It seemed she was finally willing to lend Ryuuji an ear.

"...Sorry, Inko-chan. Sweet dreams. Now then, Aisaka."

After returning Inko-chan to her cage, Ryuuji folded his feet under himself, sitting down to square off with Aisaka. She'd finally regained some of her cool and glared up at Ryuuji as though saying, *what?* Except she still cradled the plate, continuing her fried rice feast.

"You can keep eating, just listen. The thing I want to say is, basically, stuff like that isn't embarrassing at all. We're second-year high school students; having one or two crushes is a given. You can write a love letter—there's nothing weird about doing that. Every successful couple in the whole world had to get through doing all kinds of stuff before they started formally dating."

"..."

Aisaka rudely hid her face with the plate she was holding as she chewed.

"It's just, well...there probably aren't many people who'd screw up and get the wrong person's bag—or forget to put the letter in the envelope in the *first* place," he said.

"That's enough!"

BAM! Aisaka hit the table with her fist, lifted her face, and thrust the spoon at Ryuuji.

"Everything you've been saying sounds real convenient for you, doesn't it? I'll have you know—back then, I was debating whether or not to put the love letter in at all. When I opened the bag and was thinking about what to do, that's when *you* came along and made me lose my cool. I had to hide it in a hurry, so, I threw it in. And then it turned out to be your bag..."

"A-Aisaka...you've got rice plastered all over your mouth."

"Shut! Up!"

"Uh..."

Her sharp gaze grew increasingly dreadful, glinting like the honed edge of a blade. Faced with that, Ryuuji lost track of what he was trying to say.

It seemed that now that her stomach was full, her power had fully recharged. *Humph*! Sticking her chin up arrogantly, she stopped Ryuuji in his tracks with the eyes of an assassin. Her energy and brutality revived, the Palmtop Tiger's ferocious snarl was low and long.

"Takasu Ryuuji...if you'd just obediently handed over your bag when I told you, it wouldn't have come to this. Just how are you going to make it up to me? How are you going to erase your memory of it? How am I supposed to keep on living when I'm this embarrassed?"

You're going back to that subject again? Ryuuji put his head in his arms for a moment. Then he said, "Like I told you, it's nothing to be ashamed of! Look, just wait!"

He was desperate.

He dashed momentarily from the living room to his bedroom and returned carrying an armload of stuff. He piled all of it in front of Aisaka's eyes. Countless notebooks, paper scraps, CDs, sketchbooks, and even a secondhand MiniDisk player he bought once. If this was what it took, he'd show her. He'd show her everything.

"...What is this?"

"Just look at it. Look at any of it."

Tsk. Clicking her tongue, Aisaka took one of the notebooks nearest her hand, as though it were bothersome. She flipped through the pages until her fingers stopped. Her face distorted unpleasantly as she looked from the page to Ryuuji.

"What is this, really? What're you trying to pull?"

"Do you know what that list is? Bet you don't, huh? That's a playlist I made in case I ever got to put on a concert for the girl I liked. And there're four sets, for each of the four seasons. Of course, I also made an MD."

And here, he turned on the MD player. He stuck the earphones right into Aisaka's unwilling ears. A faint sound played—the summer concert's first song.

"And then around the time I made this, I also made this note, which had the theme: 'What would I get her for our first Christmas after we started dating?' I settled on perfume. More precisely, an eau de toilette. I even narrowed down a list of brands and got the prices from the stores selling them. I researched everything and wrote it all down... What do you think? I'm always doing stuff like this."

"Talk about gross!"

Aisaka tore out the earphones and flung them back, as though they were dirty. They thwacked Ryuuji, but he didn't even flinch.

"Of course it's gross! But even though you know about this, I wouldn't ever think about *killing* you! What's wrong with liking a girl, huh? Until I work up the courage to tell her how I feel, all I can do is fantasize... Which is really pitiful, but... but I still don't think it's anything to be ashamed of!"

Truthfully, it *was* a little embarrassing, but he still spoke those words—and at that moment, it happened. He'd been keeping something hidden behind his back, to keep so Aisaka wouldn't see it. Now, as he moved around, he lost his balance—and it slipped, falling right down onto Aisaka's lap.

"Ah! Oh no..."

"What's this...? An envelope?"

He rushed to get it back, but he was one step behind her small hands. His own hand writhed as it danced uselessly through the air.

"From Takasu Ryuuji...to Kushieda Minori-sama... Kushieda Minori-sama?!"

"Th-that's... Wait, wait a second, that's not—!"

"A love letter?! And it's...to Minorin?! From you?! To Minorin?! This too?! And this?!"

She left him no room for denial. He'd been satisfied just writing that letter; he'd never planned to actually send it. But now, it was fully exposed beneath the bright fluorescent lights.

"Whoa...! You and Minorin... Blech! Tell me it's not true! You insolent...!"

"A-are you really in any position to say that?! What do you mean 'blech'? Besides, you're the one who likes *my* friend, Kitamura."

"...Shut up. Do you still not get that I told you to forget about it? You sure are dead set on being dense."

"You're the one that's being dense!"

They fought loudly over her picking up the wooden sword, over him trying to get rid of it, then over whether she would hit him—or rather, who would hit whom.

"Hah!"

Ryuuji came back to himself. Before he knew it, the signs of morning light began appearing outside the window. "Oh no, it's already four..."

It was about time for Yasuko to come home from work. Having Aisaka in the house would be bad. Having Yasuko scold him was a depressing idea, but more than that, he wanted to avoid anyone seeing Yasuko say, "Ryu-chaan, your mother is *uguh uguh waaaah*." She began to wail.

And if the morning paper comes, the landlady downstairs will get up and might come complain about the noise... No, she might already be awake, and just waiting for the right moment to complain. The color of Ryuuji's face suddenly changed. *Actually, that's really likely. That's bad—if we're thrown out now, we won't have enough money for a move... And last month, we (Yasuko) used up (on her own) way too much of our savings on a flatscreen TV...*

"A-anyway! Anyway, please. I'll never say anything about what happened to anybody. I won't act like you're stupid, either. Honestly, we're in the same boat, now! So, come on, just tell me that's good enough."

"...I can't."

"Why. Can't. You. Go! Home! Please. Go. Home! My sick mom is going to get back..."

In one sense, she really did have a disease. He wasn't completely lying. But...

"No! I can't trust you, and also... and also..."

Suddenly, like a child, Aisaka curled up and held her legs. She sat down in the middle of the living room. She rubbed her cheeks into her knees, tracing words into the old tatami mats. "...Hey, that...love letter... I wonder if—you don't think it's too early to send one, right?"

Now she was asking for love advice! *Arrgh!* Ryuuji tore at his hair. "W-we can spend plenty of time discussing stuff like that— *next time*! So! Please! Go! Home! I'm begging you!"

"...You mean it? You really will give me advice next time?"

"I will. I definitely will. I'll do whatever you want, I'll help with whatever you want. I swear."

"You'll help? With anything? For me?"

"I will. I will, I will, I will. I'll do anything."

"*Anything*, right? You said *anything*, right? Like a dog, you'll do it? Like you're my dog, you'll do anything for me?"

"I will. I'll do it. I swear. Whether it's as a dog or whatever, I'll do it. So, *please.* Let's just leave it at that? Okay? *Okay?*"

"Okay...I guess I'll go home."

Seeming to finally accept those terms, Aisaka grabbed her wooden sword and stood up. When he looked very closely, he noticed tiny shoes discarded by the window. *She really did break in through the window, then...* Ryuuji groaned, and she cast him a sidelong glance as she carried the shoes toward the entrance.

Suddenly, she turned around. "Hey."

Instinctively, Ryuuji braced himself for even more suffering.

"Do you have any extra fried rice?"

"Huh? Ah, no... You ate all of it."

"I see. That's fine."

"You don't mean you didn't have enough to eat? That was about two people's worth. Were you that hungry?"

Without answering, Aisaka turned her back to him and put one foot into a shoe. Once again, without warning, she turned around and muttered, "...The sliding door."

"Yeah, there you go with another huge change of subject."

"I made a hole in the sliding door, but...does that cost a lot of money?"

Looking up at Ryuuji's face, Aisaka's big eyes blinked twice, three times. It took him by surprise and made him feel uneasy, so Ryuuji didn't return the look. It wasn't that he was scared— he was bewildered. It felt like this was the first time he had seen Aisaka when she wasn't angry.

"Uhh... Well...it's something I could do myself if I tried my hand at fixing it...I think. From what I saw earlier, the hole itself was small, anyway. But it would be better if I had nice paper, and around here, you can only buy shoji paper in half sheets."

"Hmm." She was still wearing an expressionless face, intentionally hard to read. "Why don't you use this? It's washi."

Aisaka thrust something at him. *Even if you say to use this...* Ryuuji thought, puzzling over the thing she thrust into his hand, *do you really expect me to use your empty love letter envelope...?*

"If you can fix it with that, then do it. If it costs money, I'll pay for it."

"Uhh, well...okay."

Without answering his question about whether she had had enough to eat, Aisaka started to don the straps of her bothersome-looking shoes, one by one. Her bent back somehow made him think...

"Hey, wait."

She didn't look happy to be interrupted. "What?"

"Just how many meals have you been skipping?"

"Why are you worried about that? It's not like I haven't been eating. I kind of got bored of the food at the convenience store... Even when I buy it I don't really..."

"At the convenience store? For all three meals? No way is that good for you!"

"In front of the station, there used to be a bento place, right? That closed down last month, right? And other than that, there really isn't anything except convenience stores, so... And the food in the supermarket delis is kind of... I don't know how to buy it."

"Come on, you can just put however much you want in the transparent container. And then you have them weigh it at the register... But what about your parents—haven't they taught you about all this?"

After she clicked her shoe strap closed and got up, he thought he saw Aisaka faintly shake her head to the side. *I've made a mistake*, he thought. Every household had its own issues, but given that Aisaka's was already mysterious, it wouldn't be surprising if her family situation was well outside a normal person's imagination. Even he had learned to handle a strange household environment as a kid. And that was probably putting it kindly. Uneasy as he was, he couldn't ask any more questions. He could only watch her long hair as she opened the front door and started to leave.

"Hey, wait! I'll walk you over! Being by yourself this late is..."

"I'm fine. It's close. And I have my sword."

"I think that makes it even *more* dangerous."

"It's really close. Bye, Ryuuji. See you tomorrow."

Turning around, Aisaka left.

Flustered, he put on his sandals and went after her without even locking the door. But when he looked downstairs from the entrance, she was nowhere to be found. She really was mysteriously fast. "I let her go home alone. But then..."

Just now, hadn't she used his first name?

Ryuuji's eyes constricted into slits, his cheeks distorted, and he glared in the direction Aisaka had disappeared. He wasn't angry—he was confused.

Well before the night ended and Yasuko returned, he finished cleaning the entire room. His speed was probably thanks to the fact he tidied up on a daily basis.

From that day forward, a cleverly cut, light pink cherry blossom remained magnificently affixed to the Takasu household's sliding door, among the myriad of other flowers.

3

A QUIET DAWN CAME OVER the Takasu household that made the commotion from the early morning seem like a dream.

After being attacked by the Palmtop Tiger, Ryuuji finally got back to sleep at five in the morning. With his growing body, the lack of sleep hit him hard, but his mouth opened wide into a robust yawn, and he willed himself from bed at his usual time. There were a lot of things he needed to get done.

Once he finished using the restroom and sink, he first needed to change Inko-chan's food. Like usual, he began by checking whether she was awake. After she responded, he removed the cloth covering the birdcage. But then...

"Good morning Inko-ch—oh!"

He drew his head back in astonishment. Inko-chan was dead.

"B-but you just answered me! Inko-chan!"

"...Nn...nng, nn..."

Nope, she was alive. She'd sure *looked* dead, flopped over at the bottom of the birdcage, but apparently, she was just laying on her side. At Ryuuji's call, she suddenly sprang up and cryptically fluffed her feathers until she bulged. She looked totally gross.

"Man, I don't get you at all anymore."

"Morning!"

He really wanted a cat or a dog, or some kind of pet that he could relate to. While he was in deep thought changing the food box, Inko-chan started to speak. "...Nk... nn... ng cha... nkochan... ngochan."

Staring straight into Ryuuji's eyes, Inko-chan was desperately trying to tell him something. It definitely had to be what she had practiced for years but had never once managed to say right. *This time, you won't mess it up, right?* he thought.

"Are you finally going to say Inko-chan...? Can you finally say it?!"

Reflexively, Ryuuji became excited. He had front row seats to the birdcage before him. Inko-chan astutely snapped her wings open. Finally, finally the moment had—

"Dung-ko-chaan!"

"You idiot!" In resignation, Ryuuji flung the cloth they used at night back over the birdcage, then stalked out of the family room. He looked brutish, but his heart was calm. Something like this could never stir his emotions. With the backbone of a man, he composed himself, then opened the sliding door to check on Yasuko, who would be sleeping.

When he was falling asleep, he'd definitely heard the front door open, so he was sure she had come home, but...

"...This is terrible in its own way," he groaned and rolled his eyes.

She was so drunk that she stunk up the room with the scent of alcohol, and for some reason, she was positioned as though she were about to do a somersault, butt sticking straight up as she slept. Thankfully, she had changed into a tracksuit. Even though she was his mother—no, precisely because she was his mother—this was too much. He tolerated her underwear showing, but this wasn't anything a son ought to put up with. On top of that, she must have given up partway through taking off her makeup. Half her face was clean, and the other half was heavily made up, as though she were trying her best to impersonate Baron Ashura from *Mazinger Z*—only her version of him was in pain and had an anguished expression.

If he had to guess, she'd tactlessly taken off her makeup while sitting at the small table by the edge of the futon. Then, in the middle of that, she fell asleep and flopped face first onto the *futon*.

"You're lucky you didn't break your neck... Hey. Don't sleep like that; it'll take years off your life."

"...Ryu...yuucha...n...n...chan..."

Not only was she in the same position as Inko-chan, she was *talking* like the bird, too.

He could feel the invisible bond between Yasuko and Inko-chan (their brainpower), as he gently lowered the bottom half of her body and straightened her out to sleep properly on the futon. Yasuko wanted her own bed, but with these sleeping habits, he knew he couldn't ever let her buy one.

He rescued the melted ice cream from the plastic bag that had been thrown into the corner and quietly tiptoed out of the room. As he gently slid the door closed, he decided to put the melted ice cream into the freezer for the time being.

Then he peeked into the refrigerator to start preparations for breakfast and their bento boxes for lunch.

"Oh, that's right." Ryuuji viciously scrutinized the contents. He wasn't mad—he had just been careless. He'd used up the eggs and bacon for the fried rice feast, which meant he didn't have them for breakfast. He had also used up all the frozen food.

"...I could just have milk for breakfast. And for lunch, I'll... make do. All I have that'd work as a side is taro anyway."

Ryuuji still had to make rice, so he decided to do something he normally considered cutting corners, which was making takikomi gohan—a simple, seasoned rice—and some quick stewed taro.

He washed the rice, then—before putting in the water— poured in sake, soy sauce, and mirin to taste. He threw in kombu seaweed he had cut into pieces with scissors, boiled bamboo shoots, and the rest of a bottle of nametake. Once he filled it with water and flipped the switch on the rice cooker, that was it. All he had to do was wait for it to finish cooking.

Then, with supernatural speed, he peeled the taro and threw it into a pot partway filled with boiled water. He washed the cutting board and knife, and by the time he cleaned up the sink drain, the boiling water had evaporated to show the tops of the *taro* he had thrown in. After eyeballing the amounts of zarame, mirin, sake, soy sauce, powdered broth, and mentsuyu to put in, all he had left to do was leave it alone. If he turned the heat to low to avoid burning the taro and waited until the broth only just finished boiling off, it would naturally turn into nikorogashi. He had never looked up the proper way of making the salty-sweet, potato-like dish, but it was always delicious when he made it like this.

It hadn't even been thirty minutes since he woke up. He had tons of time left. Ryuuji poured the rest of the milk into a cup, turned on the TV, and sat down on a floor cushion.

He would have his brief breakfast while watching morning variety shows. Although his eyes and ears were absorbed in a report of the soccer match from the day before, he sat and unconsciously polished the dining table with a cloth until it sparkled.

His team seemed to have won; ignoring that he'd only had milk for breakfast, the morning was going pretty well. Though it would have been nicer if there had been bright sunlight coming in through the window, like in years past. He looked out the window from within the dim room and sighed. But then...

"Gah!"

He was startled by the sudden ringing of the phone. Something must have happened to one of their relatives for it to go off so early. In any case, he couldn't disturb Yasuko (who, despite appearances, was the sole breadwinner) while she slept. He hurried to the receiver and picked it up.

"Yes, this is the Takasu—"

"YOU'RE LATE! What do you think you're doing?!"

Without thinking, he hung up.

What do you think you're doing? The words echoed in his mind, and he thought, *I'm just going about my day, that's what.* With his mind blank from the unexpected scolding, he made the mistake of diligently answering the phone when it rang a second time.

"Yes, this is the Takasu—"

"You just hung up on me, didn't you?! Do I need to come over there and go on a rampage again?"

Reflexively, he thought, *That wouldn't be good.* His landlady hadn't come to complain, but for a little while now, he'd heard the sound of a broom sweeping stormily outside the front entrance. His landlady was probably waiting to catch Ryuuji leaving the house to complain. He was marked.

Only one person came to mind who could make such wicked threats.

"Aisaka... Taiga... Tch."

In other words, the ferocious and nefarious Palmtop Tiger.

"If you don't want any trouble, hurry up and get over here! What're you up to? Do you plan to break your vow that fast? I can't think of a single reason why you'd think that's a good idea."

"Sheesh. By vow, you don't mean..."

"You said you'd do *anything* I told you, like a *dog*, didn't you? You *swore*, didn't you? So hurry up! Get over here right now. Starting today, you're coming to my house before school, every morning."

"...Hold on, wait a second. That thing yesterday...y'know, *that* thing, right? When I said I'd help you, I meant that—that I'd give you advice about Kitamura, that's what..."

"Tsk." He heard the click of a tongue packed full of irritation coming from the other end of the line.

"You're the one who said you'd do anything. Anyway, just come over. When I say I'm going to do something, I always do it. Though in this case, I'm not telling you what it is."

It seemed like she was in a really bad mood. Her voice resonated with sinister tones, like the jeer of an oni bellowing from hell. It made Ryuuji's eardrums quake. Saying anything to her over the phone when she was like this wouldn't do any good.

"W-well... I guess I'll come, but...I don't know where your house—"

"Come to the window."

"Huh? The window? If I can see your place from the window, that means—AHH!"

Phone in hand, he crossed the sadly small living room. From the shadows next to the window, he threw his head back in surprise at what he saw outside. From here, all that could be seen were the upper-class condos, but on the second floor, in a perfectly visible window...

93

"What's with that weird pajama top?" said Aisaka Taiga. She was watching him through the condo's window, a fashionable phone in one hand and a deadpan expression on her face.

"Uh, stop! Don't look at me!" Ryuuji tried to cover up Yasuko's "snuggly wuggly" heart-covered cardigan with both his hands. He had put it on because of the cold. His face turned into an ogre's, but he wasn't angry—he was embarrassed.

Her face distorted, too. She yanked her expensive-looking curtains shut. "I didn't want to see it in the first place! Hurry up and come, you mutt!" Aisaka insisted. But Ryuuji still had some things to do.

"Just wait a second! I just need ten minutes!"

"What for?"

"The takikomi gohan I'm making for lunch isn't done yet!"

"..."

Then, from the other side of the newly silent line, he heard the faint but intense sound of a rumbling stomach. It was so loud, he couldn't pretend he hadn't heard it.

"...D-do you want some, too?"

She kept quiet for a while, but eventually, the upper-class condo's curtains opened by about ten centimeters. Still refusing to utter so much as a word, Aisaka nodded in response.

Yasuko, Inko, and now Aisaka.

It seemed the number of mouths Ryuuji was in charge of feeding had increased by one.

It was the first time in his life he had seen an auto-locking door.

The air surrounding the white marble entrance was cooler than outside. It was mysteriously quiet. He felt as though he were being watched.

He felt so out of place that his eyes took on an imposing and dreadful look as he glared at the mysterious machine before him. It was in a marble stand at about hip level. It had a button, a keyhole, and something that looked like a speaker. There was an automatic door that continued to lead inside, but when he stood in front of it, it made no sign of opening. On his immediate right was the management office, but a note saying "cleaning in progress" indicated that it was deserted. He was sure that he needed to do something with the machine in order to enter the Palmtop Tiger's pen, but he didn't know what. Then a voice interrupted his silent pondering. "Good morn...ing...?"

A young woman opened the door. Even while greeting him, she watched him with a suspicious, questioning look.

"G-good morning."

Ryuuji uneasily lowered his head and slipped through the cracked door. He felt apprehensive entering this way, but no one challenged him.

He went into the elevator and pressed the button for the

second floor. When the door opened, he found a carpeted hall-way like the one he'd seen in a hotel during a school field trip.

As he wondered what the rent for this must be like, he real-ized he'd forgotten to ask for the room number. But his anxiety immediately dissipated.

There was only one door in the hallway ahead. It seemed that the Aisakas' place took up the entire second floor.

"She's rich. Maybe the rumors are true, then... Her dad might actually be a mobster."

Deep in thought and just a little nervous (even if it were Aisaka, it was still a girl's house), he rung the doorbell. But there was no sign of anyone coming to answer, and after a second ring, there was still no response.

There was still time to get to school, but time wasn't infinite. Remaining hesitant, he gently tried to open the door.

He inhaled sharply. It opened.

"G-good mornin-ng...Aisaka! It's Takasu!" He peeked inside and called out, "Heeyyy," but of course no one answered. "Heyyy, heyyyy," he called again, trespassing through the marbled front entrance.

"...Excuse me...I'm coming in! Is that okay? I-I'm coming in now, okay?"

She'd told him to come—and so he had, out of coercion. Why was he just standing around? Although he was afraid of run-ning into anyone else, especially her father, Ryuuji timidly took off the loafers he had just shined and stepped up onto the hallway flooring in his socks.

As Ryuuji continued inside, he looked around and breathed out a gasp, "Whoa..." From the white wallpaper to the beige flooring and recessed lighting, everything possessed an elegance completely divorced from ordinary rentals. Ryuuji, who actually rather liked interior design, was enthralled. He quietly opened a clouded glass door.

"Ooh! Ooh?"

First, the admiration. Then, the stench.

His admiration was for the living room, over twenty tatami mats in size. The white rug, the light gray sofa, and then the white table and refined chairs, probably hand-picked by a designer. The south-facing window opened up to a striking view of the park trees—a view that had originally belonged to the Takasu household. The muted colors of the furniture enhanced the openness of the living room, while still maintaining a personal touch. It displayed the taste of a professional. Although the glass chandelier showed modern style, it was exquisite. But strangely, there was only a sofa and a chair for one. For a living room this big, it would have been normal to have five or six people's worth of furniture.

And then the stench—

"It has to be that..."

It was coming from the refined island kitchen.

Although the sink was large, it was piled high with what might have been a fixed installment of dirty plates, bowls, and other dishware, all submerged in filthy water. Just imagining what was going on inside the drain made his body shiver. On top of that, the stainless steel in the kitchen was clouded, but that wasn't the worst of it.

"Whoaa!"

Here and there were patches of black mold. It was so widespread that he couldn't help but feel like collapsing in agony. He was drawn in. As he stumbled forward, he made the mistake of swiping the kitchen counter with a shaking pointer finger. Naturally, the sensation he felt could be described as slippery, or slimy, or...

Unforgivable.

Something like this was completely unforgivable. It was a desecration of the kitchen. It was a desecration of daily life. How could it be that while some people put in the effort day in and day out to keep a narrow, terribly tiny, totally dark kitchen like the one in his two-bedroom apartment clean enough to eat off the floor, *she* had this amazing streamlined kitchen and let it get so... so...!

"AISAKAAAAAAAA!"

Almost flying, Ryuuji started to run. After seeing a sight like this, he couldn't stand idly by.

"Let me...somehow... Just let me...CLEAN THIS KITCHEN!"

Ryuuji felt as though something inside him were about to burst open. Veins popping, he stalked around the living room like a bullet, but he couldn't find Aisaka. Then, eyes sparkling dangerously with excitement, he discovered a sliding door.

"This is it!"

He forcefully threw open the door and...

"...Oh."

He had been completely right. But somehow...it was a complete failure.

Aisaka Taiga was there.

With things so placid, Ryuuji instinctively shut his mouth and held his breath.

It was a quiet room with a high ceiling, and curtains hung from the north facing windows. Frilly dresses were strewn about here and there on the pure white carpet. In one corner of the room, there was a desk and a chair, which were naturally also pure white, and at the center of the room was a bed with a canopy of white lace.

It was Aisaka Taiga's bedroom.

Aisaka herself was curled up, sleeping quietly alone in the middle of the bed. Her long hair was scattered over the sheets, and she seemed to be sinking into the mattress, guarded by lace.

The phone receiver was at the head of the bed, and the Takasu household's window was just visible through a crack in the curtain.

"...You fell back asleep."

Only the susurrations of her even breathing quietly reverberated through the bedroom.

Unable to come closer, Ryuuji just watched Aisaka as she slept. It wasn't like he wanted to watch her, but he just couldn't take his eyes off her.

She was bundled in baggy pajamas, which made her already thin and dainty limbs seem even more petite. Her high cheekbones were currently at peace and seemed transparent, as though they had been shaped from water that could evaporate at any moment. Her small nose, her half-open small mouth, her long closed eyelashes... Aisaka Taiga quietly sunk into the ocean of sheets with only her breathing to indicate that she was alive.

This wasn't his lively classmate gone to sleep, but a scene from a made-up fairy tale world.

She's like Sleeping Beauty, he thought, somewhat girlishly, but then corrected himself.

No, this wasn't a princess.

She wasn't a princess—she was the doll the princess had forgotten. It would open its eyes if it were just lifted up, but because it was forgotten, the small doll continued to sleep.

The bed the doll was sleeping in, this room, this house, they too belonged to the princess, not the doll. That was why everything was too big. That was why nothing was the right size for her.

But Aisaka was a person, and this house was Aisaka's house— wait a minute, what *had* happened to her family?

Ryuuji spun around, looking at the house that had once again fallen silent. He squinted his eyes. A single chair. One sofa. Aisaka was the only one here. *Your family?* he asked silently, and Aisaka seemed to shake her head from side to side as she slept alone.

He looked at his wristwatch. There was still time before they needed to go to school.

Somehow managing to avoid waking her, Ryuuji quietly left the room. He closed the door without making a sound. If she weren't awake to go to school at the last minute, he would get her up then.

Once he had put some space between him and the quiet bedroom, Ryuuji slowly took off his school jacket and rolled up his sleeves.

"Right!"

The grungy, custom-fitted kitchen towered before his sharp gaze. He had fifteen minutes. Man versus filthy stainless steel. The best-of-one match began in earnest...

When Aisaka Taiga woke, an unbelievable scene unfolded before her.

She saw Takasu Ryuuji, who declared, "I'm still working on it. I'll need to do a lot more tomorrow." Behind him were half a year's worth of dishes and a thoroughly cleaned stainless steel kitchen.

And then, she saw takikomi gohan and instant miso soup for breakfast.

Then he showed her a hearty bento box, saying, "The food inside is the same as breakfast, but I'm glad I brought a lot."

All of it was for Aisaka Taiga, who had accidentally fallen back asleep.

◆ ✳ ◆

"I had you come here specifically because I *didn't* want to be late, so why did you let so much time go by? Is there something wrong with you?"

"What?! I told you to hurry up and eat faster, didn't I?! You're the one that kept her mitts on the bowl and kept asking for seconds!"

"You were dumb enough to make breakfast, even though I never asked for it, and letting some of it go to waste would have been pitiful, so I ate all of it for you. Why don't *you* thank *me*?"

"That's it. Give me back that bento."

"Shut up! Don't come near me, you dirty-minded dog."

"You...give it back! You better give it back! And give back every nice thing I ever did for you!"

"Shush. Go rot in hell."

"P-people who tell others to rot don't get to have takikomi gohan!"

As they briskly walked to school side by side, a fierce battle developed between Ryuuji and Aisaka. The two made a commotion all along the sidewalk as they strode beneath the radiant, new green leaves of the roadside trees. They were first-rate nuisances.

In an attempt to steal the bento from the drawstring bag hanging from Aisaka's small hand, Ryuuji attacked from above. Aisaka dodged and, with her small stature, quickly scuttled off to put distance between herself and Ryuuji. Not wanting to become involved with the two, the passersby averted their eyes from both the high schooler with a dreadful look in his eye and the petite beauty who seemed to ignore him as he gave chase.

"C-could you be any more ungrateful?! Jeez! And I even cleaned your kitchen for you! Well, I mean, I'm not totally finished, but *still*."

"I told you, I didn't ask for that."

"Hey, you know what was the worst? The water in the sink was totally rancid! The drain was full of slime, covered in mold, and stuffed with rotting food scraps. It looked like hell on Earth... How could you endure the smell? Just how long did you leave it all sitting there?"

"For about half a year."

"...Are you even human?!"

He whipped out his finger to point at her, but Aisaka remained expressionless. "I wouldn't know anything about that," she said and briskly walked away, leaving him with just those words. Deep down, he knew that it wouldn't do him any good listening to someone like that, but he couldn't abide the thought of leaving that kitchen as it was. After one glance at that filthy water, Ryuuji just couldn't leave it alone. He wanted to make it pretty, he wanted to make it clean, he wanted to make it easy to use—those desires reared their head. He couldn't restrain himself.

"Guess it's my vice, huh?"

Muttering to himself, he followed behind Aisaka—he had no

other choice, after all, as they had to use this same road to get to school. Ryuuji took a glimpse behind him.

"More importantly, when we get to school, you're going to bust your butt working for me. Because I won't forgive you if you slack off." After giving him that warning and a sobering gaze, Aisaka snorted.

Ryuuji increased his pace. Like he was going to let her get away with saying that. "You know what, why should I help someone with that kind of attitude—oof!"

He ran into Aisaka, who had suddenly stopped walking, causing him to take an elbow right to the gut.

"D-don't just stop like that, you idiot!" he complained, foul-tempered and painfully close to fainting. But Aisaka's gaze wasn't directed at Ryuuji at all.

"Minorin! You waited for me again?"

"You're late, Taiga. I was just about to go on without you again today."

"...Hey!" Ryuuji said. He stopped in his tracks, dangerously close to swooning. Across from Aisaka, Kushieda Minori stood at the corner of a large crossroads.

With a touch of sunburn on her cheeks and a glitter in her cute, round eyes, she wore an innocent smile while she wildly waved their way. In the morning sun, her hair sparkled radiantly; the hem of her skirt danced in the wind...but then her hand stopped in surprise. Her smile disappeared. Instead, her eyes opened up wide.

"Whaaaaaaaaaaat! Huh? It can't be—*no way!*" she said.

"What's wrong, Minorin?" Aisaka said.

"M-my ear..." Ryuuji groaned.

She shouted in a shrill voice, fervently pointing back and forth between Ryuuji and Taiga, as though verifying they had indeed walked side by side on the way to school.

"Don't ask me what's wrong!" Minori went on. "Uh, uhhh... so that's it! I had no idea you and Takasu-kun were a twosome and coming to school together..."

"Come on, Minorin, no one says 'twosome' anymore."

"I seeee! Then what is it, that thing nowadays, it's... Ohh, I'm so muddled I can't remember what it's called! Oh, I know! Lovebirds?!"

"That's not it! We're not that! We're not coming to school together! W-we just happened to meet on the way!" He reflexively blurted out an excuse. Then he got ahead of himself and presumptuously said, "Right! Isn't that right, Aisaka?!"

He turned around with a forced smile.

"What, was it really a coincidence?" Minori asked.

"That's right," he said. "Apparently, we live really close together."

But the two girls had already paired up and were happily walking ahead. With this rare chance right before his eyes, Ryuuji refused to let it get away. He restlessly followed behind them and let his imagination work. Maybe Aisaka Taiga, aware of his feelings toward Minori, had summoned him to go to school together to set up this opportunity!

But in less than three seconds, the real Aisaka turned around and shattered his delusions of grandeur.

"Later, Takasu-kun," she said. "I'll see you in class. Hee hee, you couldn't possibly have been thinking that we would go to school together? This was just a chance meeting, after all."

"Uh...oh, A-Aisaka..." he started to say, but interrupted.

"Well then, see you later, Takasu-kun!" Minori said. "Hey, hey Taiga, yesterday on TV—"

What was on? I was watching TV last night, too... Ryuuji desperately reached out with one hand. Then, just before he could chase after them, he received one final warning.

Like I'm going to let you get there first, you cheeky mutt.

"...Ah..."

He saw the words in Aisaka's momentary glance, when she turned around one last time. Laying it on thick, just the look she gave him alone seemed to speak those words.

Faced with the eyes of the palm-sized beast, Ryuuji could do nothing but stand still. She seemed to be saying that she would totally sabotage anything between him and Minori until things went well with Kitamura.

Then, a pitiful thought slipped unbidden into his mind. *But even without any interference, dating Kushieda is a wish that would never come true...*

No. If he thought like that, he'd be Aisaka's dog forever, and it would all end there. That thought conjured up absolutely horrible images of the future to come...

As he watched the two girls shrink into the distance, both of Ryuuji's eyes narrowed into slits. *Bring it on. Don't underestimate me.* After getting trampeled and stomped on, he was starting to get fired up.

I'll get Aisaka and Kitamura together and then I'll get close to Kushieda.

THE PLAN WAS SIMPLE.

They were currently playing basketball in PE class. PE was split into two halves, male and female, and each group played games on opposite sides of the gymnasium. However, until they finished preparatory exercises, they were co-ed. They would get into groups of two, stretch, and pass the ball for ten minutes.

The PE instructor didn't even care who they paired with. Everyone always paired with their friends or whoever they wanted.

After getting into his gym clothes, Ryuuji briefed Aisaka on the plan along the way to the gymnasium.

"Well, since you don't talk to him very often, I figure we might as well start now. Pair with Kitamura. That's all there is to it."

She walked next to him, playing with the ends of her braided hair, her lips narrowed.

"Easy for you to say that we should just pair up," she said, "but...

the girls and boys never pair together. I'm always with Minorin and you always pair with Kitamura-kun. I wouldn't suddenly ask him to pair up—not even on pain of death would I..."

The end of her sentence trailed off. Ryuuji waved his finger at her reproachfully and began to announce the plan he had proudly concocted.

"That's the point. Listen, if you want to make it seem casual, like you paired up with him by happenstance, you just need a little finesse. To start, I'll pair with you, Aisaka."

With a doubtful look, Aisaka looked up at Ryuuji's face. "... And then?"

"Then, out of necessity, Kitamura will pair with someone else, right? Then during warm-ups, I'll casually throw the ball and 'accidentally' hit whoever he paired up with. They probably won't get hurt, but I'll make a big deal about it and take them to the nurse's office. Then, who would be left over?"

"...Me and Kitamura-kun."

"Right? Then you'll be like, 'Oh well—guess the people who are left over have to be partners!'"

"Were you just making fun of me? I'm not stupid. Like, would that even work?"

"We'll make it work. Where there's a will, there's a way."

They put on their gym shoes and lined up with the other students around the PE teacher.

"Let's play some games of basketball," the teacher said, like he did every day, then gave his customary explanation of the procedure.

"So, let's start with preparatory exercises. Why don't you start to pai—"

"Hey, Aisaka!"

"I'm here! Let's pair up, Takasu-kun!"

"Right, let's pair up!"

"Pair up and spreaaad out. Seems like we've got a couple of real eager beavers today..."

Moving quickly, Ryuuji and Aisaka paired together and scuttled to one corner of the gym. Frightened voices chimed in from around the room. "Wow...Takasu's really reckless..."

"He's gonna be the Palmtop Tiger's next meal..."

The two of them didn't notice. They were in the corner whispering to each other.

"Anyway, we've cleared the first stage," Ryuuji said.

"Right," Aisaka agreed, as they nodded slightly and exchanged glances.

However, because of Ryuuji and Aisaka's unusual behavior, the class started going in a strange direction. From somewhere outside the frightened group, someone piped up, "Wha—is today that kind of day? Then I'll pair with a girl, too! Someone pair with me!"

That carefree voice started a ripple effect.

"Yeah, yeaahhh—I want to pair with a boy, too!"

"Sure, it's nice to mix things up every once in a while."

"Sounds like it might be fun!"

The class suddenly worked itself into an uproar. Other than a few who vowed to protect the usual divide, the boys and girls began to mix. In order to pair up, they were practically using pick-up lines.

As a result of that...

"Maruooo! Sorry—I mean, Kitamuraaa, pair with me!"

"Hm? Ohh, no problem. I just got abandoned by Takasu, anyway."

"Urkh!" Aisaka griped and hit Ryuuji once in the back, then said, "W-wait, why is Kitamura-kun with that weird girl?!"

The girl she called "weird" was Kihara Maya-chan, who could actually be considered one of the more striking students. She was a full-bodied seventeen-year-old. She had a coat of mascara on her long eyelashes, subtle pink lipstick, and cute, light makeup that wouldn't get her in trouble with the school rules...

Ryuuji kept those thoughts to himself, however, and said, "She's not a 'weird girl,' that's Kihara-san. Anyway, she's our class-mate, so don't bad-mouth her. But this did turn out a bit different from how I expected... Wha?!"

This time, it was Ryuuji's turn to exclaim.

"Kushieda, wanna pair with me?"

The boy who had so shallowly flagged her down was originally from class A, a good friend of Ryuuji's. It was Noto Hisamitsu-kun, an incredibly fresh-faced seventeen-year-old. His attempt at fashionable black glasses was the opposite of flattering. *What's with that guy?*

As Ryuuji turned to face him, Minori said, "Okay! Let's do it!" and hopped right to Noto's side and joined him.

"Hey, that's, wha—?!" Ryuuji said. "Kushieda-san is pairing with *that* weirdo?! Really?!"

"...He's your friend, isn't he? Hmph! It's because of things like this that I call you a mutt. You didn't even account for something like this in your plan, did you?"

"You didn't exactly point it out, either!"

While they both viciously shifted the blame onto each other, the instructor's whistle echoed across the gym. At the order, everyone lined back up and started first with exercises broadcast over the loudspeaker.

Aisaka got in front of Ryuuji and swung her braids obnoxiously as she began to move. With a stare and a click of her tongue, she menaced another student when she accidentally encroached upon his space. The pitiful victim frantically apologized while giving even more space up to Aisaka.

He remembered the mystery of Aisaka's nickname. "Because of her name, and because she'll pretty much bite anyone who wasn't careful (except Minori), she was called the Palmtop Tiger," a new friend had told him. No wonder she got called a tiger when she acted like that. Did she not realize how she might come off to Kitamura, even though she was a girl?

But as Aisaka did her exercises right in front of his eyes, he reflected that she didn't really seem like a girl who could have such a ferocious nickname—what with her short height and small frame. If he hadn't known anything about her, she would have seemed like a frail beauty. Actually, when they first started school, she had been considered the prettiest new student and received an incessant stream of confessions of love. Ryuuji could definitely see why.

Even compared to other girls, her small physique was on a whole different level. The tracksuits that everyone else wore normally would drag on Aisaka, so she had to cuff the hems very slightly. Even her backside was small; her build was terribly delicate.

To be honest, even after seeing a more complete picture of her, Ryuuji couldn't help but think Aisaka was cute. Of course, that applied strictly to her looks, but when their eyes would meet by surprise, his beating heart didn't lie... But then, the sweat that oozed out of him at her glares didn't lie, either.

If she weren't such a tiger on the inside, she would even be— no, what was he saying?

"You moron," Aisaka said. "What are you spacing out for? Maybe your tiny excuse for a brain finally rotted away?"

While he was distracted by a whorl of involuntary thoughts, the radio exercises had finished.

"Yeah, just keep on talking," he retorted. "I'm way too sophisticated to stoop to the level of insults that crude."

Aisaka coldly turned her back to Ryuuji and sat down with her legs stretched out in front of her. Next were stretches.

"How did I get stuck pretending to be happy doing stretches with you?" he wondered out loud. "Now that I think about it, we don't even use the balls until the very end."

While laying on her complaints about Ryuuji's plan, she extended her slender fingers to lightly grab the tips of her sneakers. If he were going to help push on her back, he would have to touch her, with only her shirt between his hands and her skin. He hesitated for a moment, before regaining his composure.

"You sure are flexible. It would have been nice if you got to have this conversation with Kitamura instead, huh?"

"Tell me about it."

Although he was exchanging pleasantries with her, he was actually incredibly flustered. It might have been because he was thinking about Aisaka's looks, but now he couldn't help but be oddly aware of her body.

The shoulder blades that protruded from her back were warm—probably because she had been moving. The lines of her bra were just visible underneath her tank top.

I might have accidentally made all the boys in the class awfully happy, Ryuuji thought.

"It's a little... Hey, take it easy. Don't push that hard."

But with that thought, Ryuuji worried about Kushieda Minori. Like Aisaka, Minori might also be showing the faint lines of her underwear to Noto.

"Ryuuji. That's uncomfortable. Hey! That's too hard! Ow, that's too..."

Even as he pondered that, his gaze focused on the area between the nape of Aisaka's neck and the part in her hair. It might have been because it didn't get hit by the sun, but it was completely white. The back of her ears and nearby carotid area didn't have a single blemish. Her skin was smooth like marble. It was as though touching her would inevitably leave fingerprints. Just looking at it, his heartbeat sped up, and it got hard to breathe...

"Urk... Urm... Urf!"

"...Hm? What's up with you?" he asked Aisaka.

When he let go, she threw her head back momentously, like a diver breaking the surface.

"I-I'll switch with you right now... Here, you wanna switch...?" he asked.

Aisaka looked at Ryuuji with an expression he'd never seen before—she grinned. Ryuuji couldn't understand what in the world had happened. Maybe something good?

Then, a few dozen seconds later, he was sitting with his legs out and his back to Aisaka. *Don't push too hard,* Ryuuji thought and glanced back.

That's when he saw it.

From a little way off, she ran straight at him. She took off and soared.

"Hey, stop—aaack!"

Carrying more force than her body should have allowed, the tiger nearly broke his spine. A sound of sheer destruction came from his waist.

"Damn... That'll be sore for a while...!"

"I'm sore, too. Consider this payback."

After wasting each other's HP, the long-awaited passing

practice finally arrived. After enduring that jumping body slam, he felt like his lower half had been smashed to pieces, but he continued to participate in the exercises, somehow. Miraculously.

"Hurry up and do it, just like we planned earlier. Are you ready?" Aisaka moved about five meters away from him. The other students had started practicing passes, and the satisfying sounds of basketballs echoed here and there throughout the room.

Of course, their earlier plan was for Ryuuji to casually throw the ball during warm-ups and gently hit the person paired with Kitamura. But there was one problem.

They'd positioned themselves so that Kitamura's partner, Kihara-san, was diagonally behind Aisaka—or diagonally in front, from Ryuuji's perspective—but Kihara-san was a girl.

No matter how gently he tried to throw it, intentionally hitting a girl with a ball...it made him hesitate. For the time being, Ryuuji did a chest pass to Aisaka.

"Why are you still passing normally?"

Her large eyes glinting dangerously like the edge of a knife, Aisaka glared at Ryuuji.

"There's this thing called 'timing.' Hey, c'mon, pass it."

"..."

With displeasure clear on her face, she returned a sharp pass. And then, when Ryuuji took the ball in hand, Aisaka motioned at him with her chin.

Do it.

She was giving him an order.

"...Well, uh... well..."

With just the right amount of deceptiveness, he threw one more pass. Aisaka caught the ball, but her mouth distorted into a scowl.

"Hey. I'm telling you, hurry up and do it..."

Then, slowly, with a stability learned through experience, she dribbled the basketball repeatedly. *Bam. Bam. Bam.*

"There!"

"Whoa!"

She hucked the ball like a bullet, right at his face.

"Y-you..."

It was close, but Ryuuji barely managed to catch it in time. One of his cheeks twitched brutishly, but he wasn't angry. Well, okay, he was a *little* angry, but even more afraid.

"Hey, Ryuuji, hey—pass it, paaass it."

Aisaka wore one of her calm expressions. With each of her beautiful, near-on aggravating side steps, her gym shoes squeaked. Of course, since she hardly intended to receive a pass, both her hands swayed playfully. *I should show her the pass of a real man.* Ryuuji concentrated his strength into both his hands, but...

"...Oh."

He stopped in his tracks, caught off guard when Aisaka glanced away. "What're you looking at?"

Right in Aisaka's line of sight, Kihara Maya ran after her ball, as it quickly tumbled away. "Heyy, Kitamura, where do you think you're throwing that?!"

"Sorry, sorry!"

Out of all the places it could have gone, the ball hit Aisaka's feet.

"…"

She was dazed.

With an unfortunate expression showing on her face, Aisaka picked it up.

"Oh, Aisaka-san! Sorry, are you mad?! I'm so sorry, it wasn't on purpose!"

It might have been because they were both girls, but Kihara smiled broadly and waved her hands, showing none of the fear a boy would have. "Throw it here." But then she noticed that her shoelaces had become untied. Kihara quickly crouched down to fix them.

In her place, someone else called Aisaka's name.

"Heey, Aisaka! Sorry, but could you pass it over here?"

It was the honor student with the glinting glasses, Kitamura Yuusaku. As expected of Kitamura, his easy, natural attitude with girls never changed.

Screech! Like a motor all out of gas, Aisaka suddenly stopped moving. From where he was, Ryuuji couldn't see her expression, but he had a good idea. Her twisted back snapped straight as a board.

Krrik krrik krrik… Clank clank clank. Aisaka took several precarious steps, the robotic sounds practically audible. Right hand, right leg; left hand, left leg—each moved in conjunction.

She approached and found a suitable position, but she threw the ball silently, without even a "here you go" or "here it comes." No, she just threw the ball away—with an abruptness that made you want to cover your eyes.

The ball, seemingly fired at random, bounced several times. But it rolled straight ahead, right where it was supposed to go... until it rolled right into Kitamura's hands.

"Right, thanks!" he said, making a somewhat outdated hand gesture—he threw her two finger guns. The hem of his t-shirt was tucked squarely into his tracksuit, and the drawstring bottoms of his pants were cinched super tight.

Does Aisaka actually like that guy? Watching on, Ryuuji maintained fundamental doubts.

"A-Aisaka...?"

"..."

Aisaka, who actually *did* seem to like that guy, had ceased all living functions—or at least, she sure looked like it. Without answering Ryuuji, she stood in the middle of the other students' passing practice, a conspicuous nuisance. She didn't so much as twitch.

After calling out several times, Ryuuji gave up and gingerly approached her. Then, doing his best to avoid rousing her anger, he said, "Hey, Aisaka."

"..."

He gently pinched her T-shirt sleeve and softly tugged her along as he walked. Aisaka was surprisingly obedient as she followed in tow back to their starting position. He glanced at her silent face.

"Whoa...!"

Reflexively, Ryuuji was taken aback. Aisaka Taiga was grinning. It wasn't easy to notice, but you could tell if you were up close.

She had narrow eyes, like a cat with a full stomach. Her cheeks puffed up with air. Her lips pursed into the shape of a triangle, and her neck turned the color of a peach. Her earlobes got even redder. Though she didn't vocalize the sound, if you listened very, very closely, you could just barely hear her breathing out, "Heh heh heh heh heh."

She was laughing.

"H-hey, wait... Aisaka, what's the matter with you?"

"Heh heh... What? Now who's the absentminded one? You should be happy, too; it suits a mutt like you."

"I should be...happy?"

Hearing such an unexpected word, it was Ryuuji's turn to pause in between the other students. Just what was he supposed to be happy about? Despite how angry Aisaka was a minute ago, now she was in a great mood, for some mysterious reason. She swung her braids around, one in each hand. She was skipping... and dancing?

But how? Why? Ryuuji felt like he could get away with asking and while he endured being whipped by her braids again and again, he furrowed his brow and tried asking an extremely simple question.

"Hey... hey, just what am I supposed to be happy about?"

Suddenly, Aisaka exclaimed in surprise and raised her head.

"I just told you! Are you saying you forgot the goal we're working towards? Woow, just how stupid *are* you? Is your brain even smaller than I thought? Hah, it's no joking matter, if you can't follow something that simple. But I'm in a good mood right now, so I guess I can explain it for you. But will you listen? You're listening, right? I-I just practiced passing with Kitamura! Heh heh!"

She capped it off with another laugh, "Heh heh heh heh heh."

Ryuuji thought for a while, then eventually he said, "Uhhh, how can I say this...?"

"Wait. You don't mean...a mere *dog* like you is going to *complain*?"

"It's not a complaint. Sorry for raining on your parade, but are you sure you're looking at this the right way? I'm just saying. You didn't practice passing with him just now, you just tossed the ball to him *once*. And was passing practice even really what you set out to do? Didn't you want to go beyond practicing and do things like have a conversation with him and become friends?"

Huh. Some of Aisaka's sharp logic came back into her grin.

That's right. Ryuuji gained confidence and dug in even more. "And what was *that*? Would you really call that exchange a 'conversation'? You were silent, weren't you? You just tossed back their stray ball and got a, 'Thank you.' Like this."

While still cradling the ball in one hand, he used his other one to mimic the stupid pose Kitamura had made.

"Hmph!" Aisaka's spirit flashed. With all her strength, she swung her tiny hand downwards. *BAM!* She knocked the ball under Ryuuji's arm down to the ground.

With terrible force, the stricken ball flew up almost to the ceiling, and—bop! It landed directly on Ryuuji's head.

A certain someone caught the ball that bounced off him and said, "You might actually have a point, there. Whoa, looks like even a broken clock is right twice a day. Hmph. Anyway, for now, let's stick to the plan."

You can't get any more pompous than that. The arrogant Aisaka was back. She practically kicked Ryuuji up from where he had collapsed on his knees. She blamed him for being slow and re-sumed position for pass practice. Then...

"Hey, Ryuuji!"

"Whoa!"

He got a super-high-speed chest pass. He hadn't regained his balance, and instead of catching it, he took it dead on in the chest.

"Damn, that hurt!" Ryuuji cried out without thinking. But Aisaka's bright eyes twinkled dangerously, almost burning with madness. The flame was stronger than before. Her fire was flar-ing up. It seemed like her delight over that momentary, chance interaction had sparked a fire of love in Aisaka. She was being an absolute menace.

"Go ahead and do it," she said. "Stick to the plan, and this time, I'll make sure it succeeds."

"Uh...it wasn't really a plan, so much as..."

"What are you saying? It's the plan *you* came up with, isn't it?! We're almost out of time, here!"

Whatever happened, what was most important was going through with the plan.

No way can I do this. Ryuuji took a quiet sidelong glance at Kitamura's partner and shook his head. She was a girl, and even if the plan was to hit her gently, he just couldn't do it. In fact, it would be better if practice time just ran out.

That's it.

Ryuuji opened his eyes, enlightened. That was it. If he just kept on wasting time, he could stall until the end of class. Of course, Aisaka would probably be furious, but he could always try running from the consequences of two-timing her. *There was nothing I could do*, he would say to her. *It wasn't on purpose.*

"You idiot, what is taking you so long...? Ahh, jeez, even at a time like this...my nose is getting kinda...itchy..."

There was his chance! While Aisaka vigorously rubbed her nose, Ryuuji pelted her with banter, machine-gun fast.

"Hey, hey, what's with the long face? Come to think of it, you were sneezing a lot yesterday, too. Do you think it could be an infection? If not that, maybe a cold? Or could it be allergies? Maybe your sinuses got wrecked by household dust? When was the last time you cleaned? Well, it *is* you we're talking about, so I'm going to guess never. That nice rug is wasted on you. That's right, that rug—where did you buy it? I sure wish *I* had one. It wasn't made in Japan, right? Man, I'm jealous."

"Hahh?! You've got a big mouth all of a sudden," Aisaka sneered. "What are you going on about?! I don't care about any of that... Ugh! My nose... Uuuh... Ach, jeez! None of that matters right now, I'm telling you t-to hurry up... Uuuughh!"

Aisaka, her irritation growing, wiggled her nose just before...

"Hurry up, come on! Hey, hey, hey, hey! Paaaaaassssss iiiit!"

She made a low growl and stretched her arms out like a jorou spider. Her eyes told him that if he actually threw the ball to her, he wouldn't be easily forgiven.

But what was one more pass to kill time? Ryuuji made a naïve calculation and felt like he could get away with one more pass back and forth. It might have been because Aisaka's nose was still itchy, but her face distorted into a wrinkle.

"Uh, uhh... Fluh..."

"Okaaay, I'm going for it Aisaka!"

Ryuuji threw one final, strong pass. To his surprise, Aisaka threw her head back and...

"ACHOO!"

"Aaah!"

At the very same moment he threw the pass, Aisaka sneezed. The sound of it rang throughout the gym, along with Ryuuji's yell... *It wasn't on purpose.* He swore it wasn't on purpose.

But, unfortunately, just at the moment Aisaka was about to sneeze, the chest pass hit her square in the face. Aisaka flew back. The ball bounced fruitlessly and rolled away. Ryuuji just stood there, dumbfounded, for several seconds. Eventually he came back to himself.

"Sooooorry! Are you okay?! Hey!"

Flustered, he rushed over to help her, but he was shaking. It was terrible—*ah*, she had a nosebleed, she'd fainted... For some reason, the images of Inko-chan and Yasuko from that morning floated into his mind. They had both been on their sides in strange positions. And now, Aisaka was like this. *Could it be what I saw this morning foreshadowed what's happening now?* Ryuuji shook his head. How could he think such meaningless things to himself at a time like this?

"Tell me what happened, Takasu! Who got hurt?! Was it Aisaka?!"

The instructor, along with the class representative, Kitamura, had both come running over. For a moment, Ryuuji thought he could entrust Aisaka to Kitamura—but then he looked down at Aisaka in his arms.

No way!

There was a problem with her face—he couldn't show her like this! His sense of guilt becoming his strength, Ryuuji picked up Aisaka.

"I-I did something terrible! I'll take full responsibility and bring her to the nurse's office!"

Making a big commotion, he pushed that face against his body to hide it and made a mad dash for the nurse's office. After that, the only thing left was an excited commotion among the boys. "That amateur Takasu brought down the Palmtop Tiger! It was impossible to look away from, even for a second!"

Unexpectedly, they had followed the broad outline of the original plan—except that every single thing outside the outline had gone wrong.

The event had a great influence on making Takasu Ryuuji become serious.

Even though it wasn't on purpose, even though it was the Palmtop Tiger, he had still given her a nosebleed. He'd gone so far as to knock her out. Her revenge would doubtless be terrible, but even more than that, it was a guilty conscience that tortured Ryuuji.

The aim of his plan was to see them all eating lunch together. If he could casually invite Minori, who was always eating with Aisaka, and also invite Kitamura, who was always eating with Ryuuji, then Aisaka would happily get a chance to sit with Kitamura. Ryuuji would be happy, too, since Minori would be there. The plan was foolproof.

Thus, when Aisaka returned to the classroom safe and sound during lunch break, he said, "Hey, Aisaka! I know it's sudden, but do you want to eat lunch with us? I wanted to properly make it up to you for what happened at the gym. You don't mind if Kitamura and Kushieda join, right?"

Kitamura, who knew nothing about said plan, showed not even a bit of hesitation. He simply raised his hand and replied, "Yeah, of course I don't mind. It's good having a fresh face around.

Well, then—we should put our desks together in a circle. That's fine with everyone, right? Kushieda, Aisaka?"

"Yeah, yeah, that sounds great, let's all do it! Taiga, come on. Takasu-kun is asking us to. He says he wants to apologize for what happened in the gym. Hey, hey—he's quite a guy, huh?"

Minori took Aisaka's arm and dragged her in front of Ryuuji. Ryuuji held his handmade bento bag to his chest. For some reason, Aisaka kept silent. Ryuuji could clearly see the word "nervous" stamped across her strangely stiffened cheeks. *Is this girl really okay?*

Unease filled his chest, but then Kitamura made an audacious statement. "I guess we don't need four desks; we can just have two people split each one."

"You're right," Minori said.

The two next to Ryuuji then started noisily moving the desks.

"Then I call this one," Minori said and—smack! She lowered herself onto one chair. Ryuuji looked at her suddenly.

Then Kitamura said, "Guess I'll go here," and simultaneously took up a position across from Minori.

Next to Kushieda?

Or next to Kitamura?

Of course, there was only one choice Ryuuji needed to make: to sit next to Minori, to share one desk, and be right next to her. But then Minori patted the spot next to her, opened her mouth, and was about to say—*Taiga, over here, over here.*

I won't let that happen, Ryuuji thought, eyes glinting sharply. But he didn't have the courage to jump to Minori's side, so he exclaimed, "Ohh, my foot is slipping!" and faked an accident. He shoved Aisaka's back as hard as he could, sending her forward.

"......!"

It seemed Aisaka had understood Ryuuji's intent. With the momentum from the push, she stretched her small body, attempting to get to the seat next to Kitamura. In order to get her butt to properly hit the goal, she tried to modify her course, precisely balancing herself. *That's right, good,* Ryuuji thought, clasping his fist—but it seemed the force he had used to push her had been too strong. Fighting in vain, Aisaka missed the seat and ended up on the ground—almost!

"It's not over yet!" Ryuuji muttered. There was no way he would let her fall. With a frantic look, he grabbed Aisaka's hand. Then he planted his feet and—looking like a couple of competitive dancers—he twirled Aisaka's body around until he could turn-push her magnificently into the chair next to Kitamura. The remaining force nearly sent Aisaka toppling out of her seat, but...

"Hmph!"

She gripped the desk with both her arms, opened her legs in a bold stance, and somehow held on through sheer strength. When the four chair legs all safely landed on the ground, Ryuuji also made his landing.

"Hahh..." he said, collapsing naturally into the seat next to Minori. *Maybe I overdid it*, he thought to himself, but then he raised his face.

"What's wrong, Aisaka?" Kitamura asked. "If you move your

desk around like that, you'll spill your tea. You're such a tomboy."

Meanwhile, Minori was saying, "Today's side dish is! ♪ Today's side dish is! ♪ Today's side dish is what...? ♪ Oh, it's fried chicken! You say it, too, *fried*—"

Kitamura and Minori proceeded at their own pace, in high spirits, while their classmates made a commotion.

"Wasn't what happened between the Palmtop Tiger and Takasu just now amazing?"

"It sure was!"

However, that nonsense didn't reach Aisaka's ears. More amazingly, she was about to blow a fuse. Her hand shook as she tried to take the lid off her bento. While still utterly stiff and expressionless, she scratched at the box's lid. One of her eyes glinted with a dangerous fire. Asking Aisaka, who currently couldn't even manage a conversation with Kitamura, to suddenly eat a bento next to him? That might have been premature.

But, very close by, Kitamura said, "Ohh, Aisaka you have a bento, too. Was it your mom? Or did you make it yourself?"

With a carefree expression, he'd asked something that required strong ad-libbing skills. Ryuuji gripped his chopsticks, and involuntarily swallowed his breath. *You can do it, Aisaka! You can't run away now—not when you've gotten this far! Start up a casual conversation and get more intimate.* But then...

"...Hm? Me?" she said.

Her expression betraying a woman strained to her limits, Aisaka bluntly pointed her chopsticks...at Ryuuji's face.

Uhh. Ryuuji's eyes became distant. *Come to think of it...the person who made that bento...was me...*

"Huh? Takasu? Takasu was the one who made your bento?"

But wasn't it better not to admit that? No, it wasn't a matter of whether she admitted it or not...

"Eep!"

Without thinking, he made a noise. Nearly a shriek.

"What is it?" Kitamura looked over at him.

Minori, however, was looking only at her karaage.

Ryuuji quietly closed his mouth, paralyzed. Dumbfounded by his own stupidity. Come to think of it, he *was* the one who had made Aisaka's bento. The contents were exactly the same as his. Seeing something like that, what would Kitamura and Minori think?

With a shaking hand, he firmly held the top of his bento, which he hadn't opened. *What should we do?* He looked aside to Aisaka, but...that was useless. She was so completely air-headed over Kitamura that her face resembled some blank-minded animal's. Opening the lid to expose the simple contents of his bento, his eye wandered restlessly. Aisaka's chopsticks were still pointing at Ryuuji.

"Takasu? What's wrong? You don't look so good."

"Y-you think so?!" he said—and then an idea flashed in his mind like divine intervention. He could just pretend he suddenly wasn't feeling well and escape with his bento.

Then, just as he stood up, Kitamura said, "Hm? A visitor? For me?"

Suddenly, Kitamura's gaze was aimed into the distance beyond Ryuuji. When Ryuuji instinctively turned around, looking in the direction Aisaka's chopsticks had pointed—in the direction of his own head—he saw a boy who looked like a first-year student.

"Kitamura-senpai, Kushieda-senpai," the boy called out.

"Isn't that kid the manager for the first-years?" Ryuuji said.

Kushieda had noticed as well and urged Kitamura to stand from his seat with her. They stood together and chatted for a while with the boy. When they came back, Kitamura said, "Sorry! Something just came up!"

"He said we're having an emergency club meeting!" Kushieda added. "Sooooorry! They told us to gather immediately at the clubroom with our lunches! Taiga, Takasu-kun, we're going to drop out! You can invite us again any time!"

In a rush, the two gathered the bento they'd laid out before and then, with apologies, they left the classroom.

At this sudden development, Ryuuji vacantly watched their retreating backs, unable to get his brain working again. He only came back to himself once he had completely lost sight of both of them.

"H-hey! They le—" he started to say, then turned to Aisaka. "Whoa!"

She was even more upset. Aisaka Taiga was depressed. She was sunk down, holding her face in both hands as she hunched over her bento. With her back bowed in misery, her already small shoulders looked even narrower.

"A-Aisaka..."

Noticing her quiet mumbling, he listened in. With a voice that sounded as though she were chanting a spell, she said, "Why, we just, bad luck, can't follow, why, I can't accept, something like this..." She was aimlessly putting together a list of complaints. Despite being paralyzed by nerves at her seat, Aisaka had probably allowed her hopes to grow, in her own way. Was this what the phrase "at a loss for words" meant?

He couldn't leave her like this, so...

"W-we can invite him again tomorrow. Anyway, let's eat our bento."

Ryuuji tried to talk to her in a voice as bright as possible. But...

"...Tomorrow?"

Pulling back her hair, Aisaka looked up at him with two seething eyes.

"Then, you mean to say you're going to hit me in the face with a ball tomorrow, too...?"

"No one's saying anything like that," Ryuuji spoke bluntly, but then he hesitated—the glaring eyes Aisaka had trained on him were starting to tear up. *Stop, don't cry*. He felt flustered.

"But isn't that what this was? You invited Kitamura-kun and Minorin to eat together today by telling them you were apologizing, didn't you? You don't have a natural excuse for it, do you, or what—what are you saying you're going to do? I don't want it to look like it's on purpose, so I never, ever..."

"O-okay, look! Eat!"

As Aisaka was arguing, her eyelashes began to dampen, so he quickly stoppered her mouth...with the taro he had grabbed with his chopsticks.

He'd cut the taro large, just the right size for Aisaka's mouth. Unable to spit it out, Aisaka chewed on it. She chewed desperately. "...Uh, was that a little too big?" Ryuuji grew uneasy over how long it took, until finally, she swallowed it with a big gulp. Then...

"...Die..."

"You what? Don't worry, taking care of people is one of the things I'm best at."

"Idiot dog! I nearly died!"

She drank her carton of milk in a single go. *Gluuuug.* She finished drinking the carton, and when she put it down, all signs of her tears had dried up.

Finally, Ryuuji breathed in. He opened his own bento and started to eat. It was at this point that he thought, *It's probably good that Kitamura and Kushieda had a visitor.* If he had just stood up and run from his seat, who could only imagine the sorts of blunders Aisaka would have made, left to her own devices. The more he thought about it, the more he felt they lucked out.

Yup, yup, nodding as he ate, Ryuuji firmly settled on that conclusion.

"Oh...Ryuuji."

Aisaka, who had been unhappily silent, suddenly raised her face. She fixed her glare on Ryuuji.

"What?"

"...This bento has no meat in it..."

"That can't be helped. If you want to live in a house that has meat in the fridge all the time, go get adopted by somebody who can afford it."

With that, they were both at ease, and started eating their bento.

All the eyes around the room voiced silent questions as they watched the surprising arrangement, but no one dared challenge the frightening pair out loud.

A peculiar atmosphere remained in the second-year C class, but time flowed on and soon enough, the end of the day arrived. Neither Ryuuji nor Aisaka had paid any notice to the classroom's atmosphere. PE, lunch break—they had to rise above those two bitter failures; they couldn't allow the last chance of the day to escape them. Even if it were only slight, they wanted to leave some sort of impression on Kitamura's heart.

"Are you prepared? Aisaka."

"..."

"A-Aisaka. Breathe, you can breathe."

"...Pah!"

It was homeroom, right before school let out. In a corner of the tumultuous classroom, Aisaka's face was the very definition of serious. At her side, Ryuuji was just as earnest. Guilt wrapped heavily around his whole body, like Shun's nebula chain from *Saint Seiya*.

"I-I'm starting to feel nervous... I wonder if this will just be a nuisance to him."

"What are you saying that for? Trust in yourself. There's practically no guy alive that wouldn't be happy getting homemade cookies from a girl. And Kitamura has a sweet tooth. He's not the type to turn up his nose at handmade stuff—and at the very least, he doesn't seem to *not* like you."

"Y-you think so?"

Yes, he nodded at her, and finally, managed to slightly ease Aisaka's tense expression. In her tiny hands, she held a package of precious, handmade cookies that she'd made during the afternoon cooking class.

It was a class for both boys and girls, so it didn't really feel too much like a present from a girl to a guy, but there definitely were boys who wanted the extras the girls made, and there were some who specifically made cookies to give to their boyfriends.

Aisaka, working sneakily so no one could see (sometimes using Ryuuji's body as a shield), had baked slightly complex cookies with a checkered pattern. The plan was to give them to Kitamura casually, saying, *I had leftovers, so would you like some?* All this was to help make a better impression on him. But there had been an accident. Of the ten she secretly baked, six of them burned black. It was because she had made some sort of palm-sized blunder misreading the oven scale. Incidentally, in order to "destroy the evidence" she'd crammed them into Ryuuji's mouth.

There were four left over. Aisaka Taiga was betting on those four. Still, nervousness visible on her face, she held the package of cookies and clenched her fist. Seeing that behavior from thirty centimeters away, Ryuuji thought her sheer stress would cause another incident. He shuddered at that foreboding premonition.

"H-hey, listen. Don't tense up so much. Be completely casual. Don't suddenly get all careless."

"I got it. Careless, right. Yeah, carefree...freeloader...freestyle... styleless..." Aisaka continued muttering, and then...

"Okaaay, get to your seeeaaats, everyone. We're starting homeroom now!"

Her small frame jumped with a start at the teacher's voice. They mixed in with the small groups of students heading to their seats. The 145-centimeter creature walked unsteadily between the desks.

Ryuuji instructed Aisaka to talk to Kitamura as soon as the closing ceremonies were done. Chances were, the perennially busy Kitamura would go on to student council, and then when his work was done, club activities. It was hard work pretty much every day after school for Kitamura. If she were slow, he would leave the classroom immediately and be on his way.

Because of that, once this homeroom ended, she needed to hurry and call out to him, but...

"Hey, hey—hey, hey, hey, hey..."

Ryuuji quickly glanced out the corner of his eye to check on Aisaka—and gulped.

He knew she was nervous. But this was beyond his expectations. Aisaka clung to the desk with her shoulders rounded, as though her stomach hurt. Her legs were shaking violently, and her face had past the realm of cute and was now the pale white visage of an ogress.

"Oh, what a lovely aroma we have in the classroom, today!" said their teacher. "I believe I detect sugar, wheat, butter... Oh, right! You baked cookies in class today, didn't you? I'm just *mad* for cookies, myself. Ha ha ha, it's really nostalgic... Back when I was with my host family in England..."

"...Tsk."

Aisaka was so wrapped up in her nervous frustration that the teacher's useless chit-chat earned a stern click of her tongue. Sensei with the rose-colored glasses, as usual (Koigakubo Yuri, single, twenty-nine). The pigeon-toed teacher (Koigakubo, single) was shaken by a jolt and glanced fearfully down at Aisaka.

"Let's not cluck at teachers, okay?" she said, trying to provide guidance.

Those around Aisaka began to tremble, and maybe her stubbornness was to blame, but she kept on with a...

"...Tsk."

"L-Listen here, now! A proper young lady doesn't...you understand what I'm saying, yes?"

"...Tsk."

"Ahh, words just don't reach some students' hearts..."

At this rate, they'd soon be dealing with an awkward scene that left the teacher covering her face in her hands and weeping over Aisaka's rudeness. She shouldn't have escalated things past the point where she could emotionally handle them in the first place. Yeah, there might have been reasons why she was single.

"Teacher!" Kitamura stood up, rattling back his chair. "As it seems like this could go on for a while, will you entrust me, as the class representative, to settle things this one time?! Please, there are people with after school activities; we can seek a proper course to resolve this issue tomorrow morning!"

In other words, *I'm busy, so could you please end homeroom?* But the unmarried person (Koigakubo, homeroom teacher, no boyfriend in seven years) tilted her head to the side quizzically.

"...I don't exactly get what you're trying to say..."

He hadn't gotten through to her at all. Reflexively, Ryuuji also felt like making a fool of himself. But that was Kitamura's role as Maruo and thus, he stood firm on both feet and said, "... Tomorrow is fine arts—so, be sure you don't forget anything! Rise! Bow! Goodbye!"

"Goodbyyyee," everyone said in a chorus, followed by, "Let's go home, let's go home."

They ended homeroom on their own. The unmarried person also (almost) seemed fine with it. She obediently left the classroom but sobbed a bit as she said, "Maybe I'm not cut out for this line of work..."

"A-Aisaka—"

Ryuuji stood up and followed Aisaka with his eyes. Aisaka stood up quickly.

"Awah!" Flustered, she dropped her own bag from the top of her desk.

How clumsy can you get? Ryuuji turned to look for Kitamura.

"Ohh, it's already so late... I'm going to get in trouble with the president again."

Lightheartedly holding his shoes, Kitamura started quickly running to the classroom door. This was bad. They needed to catch him before he went into the student council meeting. After that, there wouldn't be another window to catch Kitamura by himself. Panicking, Ryuuji rushed to Aisaka.

"You don't need shoes! Hurry up and go stop him!"

"Ah, uh...! Ki. Ki—Ki..."

What are you doing? He scratched his head. Aisaka stood up, but though she reached a hand out towards Kitamura's back, she couldn't call out his name. *Kitamura-kun.* It seemed she had magically forgotten those five syllables. Her face distorted, as though she were about to cry, and she opened and closed her mouth.

"Ugh, he just left! We're going to run!"

"Ah—okay!"

Ryuuji gave Aisaka's small back a strong hit and forced her into a run. He followed after her with long strides. This clumsy girl—if he left her alone, he didn't know what stupid thing she might do.

Holding the package of cookies to her chest, Aisaka jumped out of the classroom to pursue Kitamura. Ryuuji went with her. Down the hallway, they saw the back of their target for a moment as he turned a corner.

"Over there! After him!"

As the flow of students began heading for the entrance opposite their direction, Aisaka increased her speed. He thought it would be difficult for her to part the sea of people as they were heading home, but...

"Get out of my way!"

With just those curt, violent words, the people standing in Aisaka's way exclaimed:

"Look out! It's the Palmtop Tiger!"

"Everyone get out of the way! Danger, incoming!"

They parted themselves to the right and left as though she were Moses. After she'd passed by, the people divided in her wake began to return to their places, until...

"Sorry! Please let me through!"

At Ryuuji's very normal words, they panicked again.

"Look out! It's Takasu!"

"The second villain is coming through!"

Thus, it was another Moses-moment. It seemed that word still hadn't gotten around to the other classes that Takasu wasn't really a thug. He paused in a momentary depression, but this was not the time for that; he immediately started following behind Aisaka again.

In that one moment of delay, however, he had lost track of Kitamura. He just barely glimpsed Aisaka's hair as she went up the stairs. Kitamura and Aisaka were both unexpectedly fast. Mediocre Ryuuji was out of breath. Using all his strength to get up the stairs, he quickly followed them to the second floor.

But suddenly, he realized he didn't actually need to catch up with them. If Aisaka could successfully stop Kitamura, and he could just confirm that she got to him, that would be good enough.

"...Haah, haah..."

Holding his heart, which felt ready to shred apart, he stopped climbing the stairs to catch his breath. Then, he looked nonchalantly upwards—what a terrible coincidence. Reflexively, he shouted.

"Aaaaaaaaaah!"

At the very top of the stairs, Aisaka slipped trying to take the last step. *Pow!* She threw out her arms. Somehow, she had come into Ryuuji's field of vision at the very moment she began to fall.

He screamed—and a superhuman strength awakened in him.

With unthinkable speed, Ryuuji *flew*.

"...!"

He got her with a sliding catch. Ryuuji, who had jumped out onto the landing, miraculously stopped Aisaka's fall. But he couldn't stop the momentum. Still holding her small body, Ryuuji crashed into the wall.

"Guh!"

The noise he made was right out of a manga. He opened his eyes wide in pain. Then, right before his eyes, he saw a familiar package fly out of Aisaka's hands. It traced an arc through the air and fell out of the open window.

They were three stories above the ground.

What fell were the four cookies she had struggled to make.

"Eek!" he squeaked out. Aisaka, still in the position she had fallen in, reached a hand toward the window. But it was too late—they had probably already hit the ground.

"...Ah." *Aisaka*, he tried to say, but his voice wouldn't come out. He had lost his breath when he had hit his back.

"Ryuuji!"

The small voice immediately followed his. It seemed Aisaka had noticed. Her face changed color as she clung to Ryuuji. She was at a loss for words, but settled on a scowl. Like she'd been paralyzed with poison, her face froze in that expression for some time.

But, it wasn't a big deal—Ryuuji somehow regained his breath, then waved his hand to show her it would be okay. It wasn't as bad as her expression made it out to be.

More importantly—the cookies. And Kitamura. He pointed at the stairs and window in turn.

"Ch-chase after him. Pick that up..." Somehow, he managed to squeeze out his voice and push off Aisaka. He still had spirit. She had struggled so much in making them, and since he had helped get them done, he wanted to see them delivered to Kitamura, too.

She'd put in so much effort—he wanted the object of Aisaka's desire to understand just how she felt.

But Aisaka didn't even try to look where he was pointing. "Ryuuji, are you okay?! Argh, ugh, how could this have happened...?"

She was frantically feeling Ryuuji's neck and ankles, checking for broken bones. Even the violent Palmtop Tiger was disturbed when someone got hurt protecting her. His back ached, so he really wanted to stay sitting a while longer, but...

"I'm fine, so... Here, see? I'm not hurt."

Ryuuji stood up and stretched for her, forcing himself to put on a healthy face. Luckily, he didn't hurt anywhere else, and he could still move his whole back. It seemed like he really was fine. Seeing him like that, Aisaka finally breathed in.

"Ryuuji...I-I..."

She stretched both her hands out to Ryuuji. Wearing an expression he hadn't seen before, she opened her mouth to continue speaking but was interrupted.

"Heyyy! Which student just threw something out the window? Hurry up and get down here, *right* now!"

"Guh." She shut her mouth. It was the voice of an infamously strict teacher, a professional guidance counselor. With that happening, all hope of getting the cookies to Kitamura was lost.

"...Bad luck. Oh well, better go down to get the cookie and get yelled at. I'm going to wait in the classroom."

"But...at least let me walk you back, first."

"It's fine, I can walk by myself. Hurry, or she'll make a scene."

He pushed on her back to encourage her to leave, but Aisaka frowned at Ryuuji and looked over several times before she finally went down the stairs.

In that time, the teacher's voice heated up even more. *It would have been good if Aisaka hurried up*, he thought. But was there really anyone in the world that could shepherd the Palmtop Tiger?

Ryuuji walked slowly, muttering to himself in a small voice, "...Heh. I used it up..."

He was thinking back to something Yasuko shared with him when he was in elementary school. According to her, she was apparently "sliiiightly psychic," and until the day of her death, she had the power to warp—no more than three times. At any rate, Yasuko had used that power twice already. Once when she was a kid, she got in a traffic accident. She was thrown twenty meters into the air, but because she warped just before crashing into the ground, she'd been fine. And then, the second time, she used it when she ran out of the house to deliver Ryuuji, heading to the man she loved (who had a magazine stuffed under his shirt). Although she didn't tell him much about it, she had, of course, safely gotten to him because of that miraculous warp.

And then, as for the last warp... "I'm going to give it to you, Ryu-chan! Your mother doesn't have anything she wants to use it for," she said. Then she went "Pah!" at Ryuuji, who was a kid back then, and gave it to him. She said, "If something dangerous happens, you have to use this power and come back to me."

Instead, Ryuuji had used it to save Aisaka. He'd wanted to use it several times before, when he was running late—but it was good he'd saved it.

Sorry, Yasuko, he thought.

"Are you sure you're okay?"

"Completely. We've already had this conversation a hundred times."

"Then, that's okay... Even if you are a dog, I wouldn't be able to sleep right if you really got hurt." Softly muttering, Aisaka placed her forehead against the window's glass. *That's nice, coming from someone who came to kill me with a wooden sword,* Ryuuji nearly retorted, but somehow kept his mouth shut.

Since she had picked up the cookies and come back to the classroom, Aisaka's voice had no strength in it. Her spirit seemed extinguished.

The silent after-school classroom was deserted—only Aisaka and Ryuuji were there. No one could see this profile of the Palmtop Tiger except for him.

"...We've made mistake after mistake. Not a single thing went right."

She talked to herself, voice seemingly bereft of the energy it had earlier that day, hoarse and fading.

"It's only been one day since we started the plan, right? It figures it wouldn't go perfectly."

"...Is that all that's wrong? If I didn't make those mistakes, it might have almost... And I got you hurt. Not a single good thing came out of this...I don't want to do it anymore."

Aisaka turned her back to the window, slid down, and

squatted. She cradled her knees and sat on the ground by Ryuuji's feet while he stood beside her.

She pulled at her long hair with her fingers. As though wanting to hide her expression, she buried her face in her hair. "In the seventeen years up until now, I never realized...but, I finally get it. I'm a klutz."

The hands pulling on the hem of Ryuuji's pants were like a child's.

"Even you...even you think that, don't you, Ryuuji? You must be so tired of me—of this hopeless klutz."

When he looked down, Aisaka stared up at him. Their eyes met. She pushed her cheeks against her cradled knees, and her thin eyelids fluttered, as though from some hidden hurt.

Her usual aggressive intensity was subdued, replaced by a rush of self-hatred that seemed to overflow from her eyes.

"During PE, that was my bad. The plan itself was flawed," Ryuuji said.

"That's not the only thing...that I failed at." Aisaka closed her eyes as though exhausted, remembering their train wreck of a day.

Third period PE. The unlucky lunch. And then that horrible failure just now.

Once she knew it was Aisaka who dropped the package of cookies, the guidance counselor apparently hadn't been able to provide much guidance, and so Aisaka pretty much immediately came back to the classroom where Ryuuji was waiting.

He was glad it hadn't turned into a big deal, but...

"...Even though I put all that effort into making them...I just... Haah."

As Aisaka muttered, he saw a small scratch on her chin, left by a sleeve button during his rescue. While touching the cut gingerly, she brought out the newly returned cookie bag from her pocket. Inside remained the scant few cookie crumbs that hadn't fallen out.

"When I wrote the love letter, I put it in the wrong bag. When I broke into your house, I collapsed out of hunger. When I played basketball, I got a ball right to my face. When I tried inviting him to lunch, he had something to do with someone else. When I baked cookies, I burned them and fell down and dropped them, and I'm just... I'm really...tired of it..."

"You forgot one. Remember the empty envelope?"

"...You're right."

He had meant it as a joke, but it came out badly. Burrowing deeper, Aisaka put her head between her knees again and remained silent.

"A-Aisaka..."

No answer.

Still sitting strangely, she curled up into a small ball, like a snail withdrawn into its shell. She didn't move in the slightest. She grabbed onto her skirt-covered knees, slim fingers faintly trembling. As her delicate shoulders tremored with her breathing, a strand of her hair slowly fell down.

I definitely said the wrong thing, Ryuuji thought. *Girls are so unfair.*

Even though she normally acted so arrogantly, and caused people so much trouble, when he saw her in this state, as a guy, he couldn't help but feel his chest ache—because he couldn't stand a sight like this. Because it was absolutely, completely intolerable.

Ryuuji scratched his head vigorously, then his eyes honed themselves to a sharp point. He briefly went back to his seat. Then he got down next to Aisaka and sat the same way she was.

"...Let's trade, Aisaka."

"...?"

He poked her shoulder; she looked up. Pretending not to notice the moisture around her eyes, he put a bare, foil-wrapped package on her knees. Then, in exchange, he plucked the cookie bag Aisaka was holding from her.

When he opened the torn bag, he found nothing but crumbs, but there were a couple pinches remaining.

"Uh, wai...Ryuuji. You know that's already been on the floor, right? A-and, uh—"

"I only got the burned ones, so I wanted to know how they turned out," he asserted bluntly. Heedless of the wide-eyed Aisaka, he took a pinch with his fingertips and tossed it into his mouth. Then...

"..."

Silence.

The burnt cookies she'd thrust into his mouth had been hot and bitter. They'd choked him and were forced on him besides, so he pretty much spat them out in disgust. This was the first time getting a real taste of the cookies she had made. But...he was pretty sure she had mixed up the sugar and the salt...

"Is... i-is it good?"

"Yeah, it's delicious!"

Aisaka's eyes, which had been trembling with worry, became round.

"Yeah, you made them really well," he went on. "It's just too bad you didn't get to give them to him. Next time we get a chance, let's try and do better."

He pulled through with the poker face of a lifetime. He urged her to eat the cookies he'd given her. Opening them hesitantly, Aisaka once again seemed surprised, and turned to Ryuuji.

"Wow...they're amazing.! These cookies turned out perfect! Are you sure? You want me to eat them?"

"I'm the kind of guy who was just going to take them home to his mom, so it's fine. Go ahead and eat them all."

The thin cookies, glazed in butter and sugar, were specially made. Aisaka spent a while staring at their perfect glaze.

"...De-li-cious! They're great!"

She stuffed them into her mouth, and her eyes opened wide.

"That's the first time I've heard the word 'delicious' out of your mouth."

"But this is amazing! They're better than the kind they sell in stores!"

"I speak from experience: things you bake at home generally *are* better than what's sold in stores. I have my own favorites, but

I think that's particularly true if you like stuff that's fresh and soft."

"It really is... Wow, these are great. Super yummy!"

As she was absorbed in eating cookies, Aisaka's profile looked exactly like that of a regular girl. *Delicious, delicious.* Her cheeks stuffed full, she licked the sugar around her lips. "If only I had tea, this would be perfect," she said quietly to herself.

Just who knew?

Other than him, who knew of this Aisaka Taiga?

It was a really strange feeling. Up until the day before, he, like everyone else, had been afraid of the "Palmtop Tiger"—and not just afraid of getting bitten, but also fearful of engaging in her world. He'd had no idea that Aisaka Taiga was this kind of person.

But in truth, she was *this* kind of person: She had a rough temperament and was either the daughter of a thug or a karate master; she was mean enough to call other people dogs but couldn't even say the name of the guy she liked in his presence; and she was unbelievably clumsy and so ashamed of her clumsiness she could get completely depressed over it and cry almost immediately. Plus, on top of all that, she was always hungry and had a particular weakness for anything delicious or sweet.

What a weird girl. She was a nuisance. A troubled person.

But Ryuuji didn't particularly dislike her oddities, he suddenly realized. He was glad he'd met her. That was the only way he could think of it. Right then, at that moment, it felt strangely comforting.

That was right. She was perplexing, maddening, and a nuisance, but when she was hurt, he wanted to console her, to a certain extent. When it came to Aisaka, he felt...

"...Hey, Ryuuji, I figured it out." She jumped up.

When he came back to himself, Aisaka Taiga was looking at Ryuuji's face from a very close distance. Even though she was small, her features were deeply set, well balanced. When she blinked, stars seemed to fall in her large, transparent eyes. They were exquisite. Even though her body was small, she didn't have a baby face at all. That realization surprised him, and a shudder ran down his spine.

Ahem, he cleared his throat. "...I-Is something wrong?!" He could only manage a strange, flustered response.

"We've been failing because *you* haven't been working hard enough! You're really a bad dog! You mutt!"

"..."

Aisaka heaved her shoulders and huffed in overdramatic exasperation. She lowered a contemptuous stare. Somehow, it seemed she had regained her spirit and, well, what could you do?

She's really irritating. What a bizarre person, Ryuuji thought. But, right now, Aisaka was faintly smiling, so...for now, he decided he would shut up and forgive her.

It wasn't a big deal.

Their homes were slightly apart from each other, but they still shared the same route home.

Up ahead, Aisaka stopped just in front of the school gate. From there, the athletic fields were visible from between the gaps in the hedges.

"What is it?"

"...It's the softball club. Minorin is there."

Minori was running energetically in the twilight where Aisaka pointed. In Ryuuji's eyes, a spotlight suddenly shone down right on her and only her.

But he understood. Aisaka's gaze didn't follow the place she indicated with her pointing finger. Instead, her gaze was focused over on the boy's division as they stretched. She had taken note of Kitamura in the middle of the group, and his undyed black hair.

Aisaka stood quietly still, right where she was. The orange sunset outlined the silhouette of her profile with gold. Even though a slightly chilly breeze blew, Aisaka's back did not budge.

It seemed that, somehow, she really, truly did like Kitamura Yuusaku.

"Hey. Come to think of it, I haven't asked you but...why Kitamura?"

Aisaka turned at the sudden question but didn't answer. She just blinked, and stared back into Ryuuji's face with her transparent eyes, colorless in the sunlight. Then...

"I'm going home first, so why don't you stay here for a little while?"

It seemed like a dodge, but it was enough for Ryuuji, because he was trying to figure out why he'd just asked the question.

"...What do you mean, you're going home first?" he said.

"You want to ogle at Minorin some more with that gross look in your eyes. You can watch her, but you shouldn't expect anything ridiculous like you being with her any time soon. I know she's beautiful. I completely understand why you chose Minorin. I'm not so cruel as that. Oh, and come at eight o'clock to make dinner. Well, then—see ya."

See ya, she says. No, it was the part about dinner—that was the real kicker... No, it was the see ya.

She left him no room for questions. She turned her back to him and started walking off by herself. Then, immediately...

"...Wah!"

She turned on the klutz power at full blast. She reached slightly uneven ground and tumbled over. Everything in the bag she was carrying flew out. Like a child, she was defenseless.

"Uggh. What is wrong with you?"

Sighing, Ryuuji ran to her. He helped Aisaka up, while she shouted things like *you're nosy* and *leave it.* Then he put the bag in her small hand and brushed off the dirt that had gotten on her skirt. That's when he noticed them. There were scars all over her defenseless kneecaps... She must have fallen countless times, over and over again, while no one was looking.

How can I leave someone like that by herself...? He sighed again. Then, he raised his head and looked at Aisaka straight in the face.

"How are we going to do dinner? I get to eat some too, right? And I get to bring some home for my mom. Oh, and your house's fridge is completely empty, I can't make anything with just that, so we've gotta stop by a supermarket. You'd better be paying for all the ingredients. Oh, also—to assault that kitchen, we'll need to buy mold killer and bleach!"

Guess there's nothing for it, he thought.

If Aisaka told him to do something, he couldn't turn her down. He understood well enough after that day and the day before. At any rate, she was stubborn, and pushy and unfair and self-centered, and her threats were nothing to laugh at. And once she decided on something, she would definitely do it. Because of that...she was someone to seriously watch out for.

Because of that...he couldn't leave her alone. There was no helping it.

Not to mention the fact that the Aisakas' kitchen island was so dirty he couldn't even dream of looking away.

"HEY. MOVE YOUR HEAD. I can't see the TV."

The head blocking half of Ryuuji's vision didn't even turn. All that he got in return was monotone backtalk. "Shut up. You can just watch from the side."

"Excuse me?! This is my house's TV! If you're gonna say stuff like that, just go back home! It's right outside the window!"

"..."

"Don't! Ig! Nore! Me!" he shouted at her, and finally Aisaka showed him a glimpse of the side of her face. From under her long eyelashes, the curved surface of her eye held a misty sheen.

"I'm watching TV. Can't you be quiet for a little while? It's things like this that make me wonder if you're even housebroken, mutt."

He gave her a cold glare. "Y-you..."

These were always the kinds of moments that made concerns

about that dreaded two-word phrase, "neighborhood nuisance," disappear from Ryuuji's mind. He leaned forward on the dining table and attempted to prod at the self-appointed head of the house, who had planted herself right in front of his TV. But then...

"Ryu-chaan, don't be so louuud." He was gently rebuked by Yasuko, who appeared from behind the sliding door, which opened with a rattle.

"Y'know, yesterday, I got in trouble with the landlady. She said that we've always been a noisy family, but lately, we've been especially loud."

"Well, it was because this... Argh! You're naked!"

At Ryuuji's voice, even Aisaka turned around with surprise on her face. Inside her birdcage, even Inko-chan made a face as she looked at Yasuko, as though gasping in surprise. All three gazes pierced into Yasuko's white skin. But she was perfectly calm.

"Am nooot. That's just how this outfit's made to look. And I'm going to wear thiiis on tooop."

She bent down in her string style dress, which was way more skin than string. In her hand was some kind of ridiculous fluffy jacket, sporting a faux leopard-fur print.

"...That outfit is way over the line."

"Hee hee! It's cute, right? Taiga-chan, whaddya think? Hee hee!" Yasuko swung the hem of her skirt around.

Aisaka looked at it with an unchanging expression. For some reason or other, Ryuuji held his breath.

"...Look there." Aisaka's small hand swiftly pointed at the center of Yasuko's rear. "Your underwear's showing."

"Aaaah! You're riiight!"

But without missing a beat, Inko-chan shouted, "But that's the good part!"

She didn't even hesitate. *How stupid. Who would listen to a bird?* Ryuuji knitted his brows as, before his eyes, his very own mother's face lit up. She was completely eating it up. Still holding onto the hem of her skirt, Yasuko made a full twirl with her panties completely showing.

"Then I guess this'll do! I'm off to work!"

With a giant smile, she jiggled her giant breasts. Then, she happily cradled her one Chanel bag (which she'd diligently saved up for) and childishly waved both her hands.

"See you, Ryu-chan, Taiga-chan. I'm going out!"

"Okay, be careful. Don't drink too much. If someone strange bothers you, call home."

"Yuuup. Oh, Taiga-chan, don't stay out too late."

"I won't. See you later."

The old iron door closed with a clunk, creating a heavy partition between the world and the Takasu household.

Simply put, their subsequent activities went more or less like this:

"Phewww. I'm having tea."

"Make me some, too. And snacks."

"Snacks? I wonder if we have anything... You know, you could do more than just chow down. Why don't you try making yourself useful and bring over some food yourself every once in a while?"

"..."

"I was just telling you not to ignore me!"

Before they knew it, Takasu Ryuuji and Aisaka Taiga had gotten completely used to each other. They acted just like family. That was only natural, however, as their lives had grown almost completely interdependent.

In the morning, in order to keep Aisaka from sleeping in, Ryuuji would pick her up from her condo. He made the bento boxes at home and brought them over, and while Aisaka was dressing, he prepared a simple breakfast.

Then, they both left home together, and after reaching Minori, they put some space between themselves. With a subtle feeling of distance, they walked to school.

Once they got there, they came up with new strategies to capture Kitamura on a daily basis. When it came time to actually execute the plans, however, they generally failed.

When they went home, they went to shop at the supermarket, and until recently, they made dinner at Aisaka's house. That was where things got problematic. Ryuuji could eat with Aisaka, but making Yasuko's dinner was a bother. Making one dinner and then going home to make another meant twice the time and effort. And he just didn't feel like making one at Aisaka's place and carrying it the few meters it took to get home.

With that in mind, it made sense for him to cook at the

Takasu household and for all three of them to eat together. They had come up with that idea on a whim and from there, it had gained momentum. Thinking back on it now, maybe he'd finally got fed up with the obligations of a double life. It might have also been because, although Aisaka's kitchen was squeaky clean, it was surprisingly hard to use. But that might have just been because he was frustrated at the dull knives and lack of plates.

Yasuko, for her part, unexpectedly accepted Aisaka as a normal fixture, and Aisaka was equally unconcerned about Yasuko's unique personality. They just ate dinner together, and whenever Yasuko left to work her odd hours, Aisaka would wave goodbye along with Ryuuji.

At first, Aisaka would walk home with Yasuko when she left for work, but because of the TV, because of the manga, because she didn't feel like it, because she was tired, because of something about Kitamura-kun, because Kushieda-san did something, or because of any number of reasons, her stays at the Takasus' grew longer and longer.

"...Ah!"

By the time Ryuuji realized it, it had already come to this.

He rubbed away his drool with the back of his hand and, in a fluster, called out across the table.

"Hey, Aisaka! Wake up!"

"...Hm...?"

At some point, it seemed they had both fallen asleep while leisurely watching TV. They were still lying around on the tatami mat, Ryuuji in his tracksuit and Aisaka in her frilly dress. It was three o'clock in the morning.

"No matter what, you can't just sleep over here. C'mon, get up and go home! You can snooze in your own bed!"

"...Nnn."

He couldn't tell if she understood or not, but she rubbed her face into the floor cushion she'd folded into a pillow and scratched at her belly under her clothes. *Jeez, you're just like an old man.* He tried to pull the cushion forcefully from under her head, but...

"Uh...mnn...nn..."

The back of her head hit the tatami mat, and she furrowed her brow for an instant. Eventually, she rolled her head around to feel out the tatami mat, and, position more or less stabilized, she once again started breathing the deep, peaceful breaths of sleep.

Beside her, Ryuuji sat with his legs folded under him. He tilted his head as he looked down at her sleeping face. Just how close of a relationship did they have? To think there would come a time when he would so naturally spend time with a girl... No, this wasn't the time to think about that. She wasn't just any girl. His opponent was the Palmtop Tiger. But was this really the same Palmtop Tiger who once roared so ferociously?

An imprint of the cushion showed on her pink cheek. Near her mouth was the hot milk she'd been drinking before falling asleep. Her hair was delicately tangled over the mats and there was not even a trace of nervousness on her peaceful, sleeping face.

Even though she was sleeping in a boy's house.

"...Hey. Aisaka... Aisaka, wake up."

In the silent two-bedroom house, the only sound was the faint hum of the refrigerator motor. It was too early for daybreak and there was a little time before Yasuko came home. Under the cloth, Inko-chan was also sleeping in her peaceful, ugly way.

"Aisaka Taiga."

Her eyelashes cast a long shadow over her cheek. When he looked closely, her slender neck quivered with her pulse. Thinking he would speak closer to her ear, he turned over her upper body. Then, suddenly, she stiffened. A mysteriously sweet smell made Ryuuji's nose quiver. This was Aisaka's scent.

"I swear, if you don't wake up...I-I'll...molest you...?"

He didn't mean it for real. The thought of really having his way with Aisaka didn't so much as enter his head. There were already other people he treasured inside his heart (Minorin...) and he didn't want anything like that. Seriously. ...But *still*.

She was just so shameless about not waking up. He wanted to shock her, and those words came out. That was it. Really, he thought she would suddenly get up and tell him off.

But she didn't respond at all. Instead, he noticed something. A single piece of straw from the tatami was stuck to one of Aisaka's cheeks. It probably prickled...but it didn't seem to bother her... It *did* bother him, though. So, purely out of goodwill...he considered just picking it off for her. With a gulp. Ryuuji swallowed his spit. Then he slowly reached his hand out...

"Ngah!"

And was thrown across the room.

"Mnn...? What are you doing...?"

"N-nothing..."

That was just way too lucky to be a coincidence. He'd collided with Aisaka's arm as she was sitting up. She'd gotten Ryuuji with a firm hook to the chin right upon his approach.

Pulling up her hair, she sat up. She raised her brows. A suspicious look lingered in her eye as she glared at Ryuuji, who'd just turned a somersault.

"...You're so gross. What are you doing, making all that fuss all by yourself? It's the middle of the night. You'll tick off the landlady."

"L-leave me alone."

If Aisaka had been awake, Ryuuji probably wouldn't be alive. He only got off this easy because she'd been sleeping.

Aisaka really was the Palmtop Tiger. The ferocious DNA that ran through her veins flowed throughout her whole body. She was a girl who lived impulsively, biting anyone she pleased, without a care as to who they might be—it was just in her aggressive nature.

Although he had learned how to get along with her, Takasu Ryuuji had just re-affirmed her identity by taking the opportunity to touch her.

Testimony #1

"I'm Haruta Koji, from second-year class C. I'm totally positive I saw it! It was when I was on the way back from club. I was thinking of getting something to munch on for the trip home and stopped by the supermarket near the station. It was definitely Takasu and the Palmtop Tiger. Takasu was carrying a shopping basket and picking out fish or something, and the Palmtop Tiger tried to put meat in and got in trouble. He was like, 'Nope, we're getting boiled fish today,' and then she put it back on the shelf. Then, the two of them bought green onion and Japanese radish and stuff, and *then*, when they got to the front of the register, Takasu was like, 'Take one thousand yen out of the communal purse.' And then the Palmtop Tiger actually listened and took out the wallet. Dude, who has a 'communal purse'? Doesn't that sound like a husband and wife thing to you?"

Testimony #2

"I'm in the same second-year class. My name is Kihara Maya. I saw them in the morning while going to school. I live on Chari Road, but there's a really luxurious new condo pretty close to school. Whenever I go by, I always think about how I want to live in a place like that—and that's when I saw them. Suddenly, who would you know but Takasu-kun comes out. And just when I was thinking 'Huh, you live here?' Aisaka-san came out like she was following him, and then she was, like, saying she was sleepy. And she was like, you should have woken me up earlier. And just as I was thinking, *No waaayy*, Takasu-kun turned around and yelled at her, 'I tried waking you up more than once!' That's, like... you know...right?"

Testimony #3

"Um, I'm Noto Hisamitsu from second-year class C. Takasu and I were in the same class our first year, so we still hang out a lot. But lately, whenever I've been thinking of going home with Takasu, he disappears. And I was like, 'What's up with that,' y'know? Yesterday, a band I like dropped a new album, so I wanted to go to the CD store with Takasu to check it out, and during lunch I tried asking, but...it was definitely weird. He said something like, 'Wait a sec,' and then says, 'Hey, Aisaka, I won't go home with you today, is that okay?' And then he goes, 'I'll be there at 8 o-clock.' Like...where? To do what? And then while we were looking at CDs, I asked him, what was *that* all about? But he was like, 'Don't worry about it,' and that was it... Talk about weird, man."

Testimony #4

"I'm Kushieda Minori from second-year class C. First off, I'm close friends with Taiga, but...I'm certain that she's hiding something from me. We meet up every morning and go to school together, but it's like...Takasu-kun is there...and he walks a little further back and pretends like he doesn't know us. They're totally a twosome. They're lovebirds. But Taiga says, 'We met by chance,' and, 'Oh? I didn't notice,' and stuff like that. Well, last year she would sleep in one out of every three days, so I think it's good she's not being late anymore, but...I don't like how she's being so dodgy with me. And when they get to school, they're always whispering secrets to each other...and I was like, wait, maybe this feeling...maybe it's envy?! Now what's that thing about the rose's thorn, and the red and white sisters...how does that go again?! Oh, I can't think of the word that's used nowadays!"

Ryuuji being Ryuuji, he was used to being the target of gossip when onlookers misinterpreted his stares. Or to put it another way, he had learned the art of not letting stuff get to him partially as an instinctive act of self-defense to keep himself from getting hurt.

Aisaka being Aisaka, she was used to everyone keeping their distance out of fear of her wild temperament and near-professional punches. She wasn't the type of girl to lend an ear to others' gossip to begin with and generally didn't take an interest in people other than herself (excluding Minorin and Kitamura).

In that way, because the two were accustomed to unwanted attention, they had for the most part failed to notice the current state of affairs—the restless class. The whispered words being exchanged. The scattered glances. And, of course, the voices of agreement.

"...I saw it too, I saw them coming out of the same condo..."

"Just before, they really were at the supermarket together."

"They're whispering to each other again..."

"Oh, they disappeared together."

"The Palmtop Tiger was calling him Ryuuji."

"Takasu being Takasu, he was calling her an idiot and stupid like it was fine."

"He said that and he came out alive..."

"The insides of their bento were the same again!"

Maybe Takasu Ryuuji and Aisaka Taiga were...

"Oh. Right."

At the tiny Palmtop Tiger's mutter, the shoulders of those around her jolted.

"What's going on?"

"Are you going to mess with her?" they asked each other. But Aisaka, now the center of the attention, didn't betray any awareness of them.

"Hey Ryuuji. I almost forgot," she said, trotting over to Ryuuji's seat by the window, completely unaware of the people around her who had their ears pricked up.

"What?" he said.

"Yesterday..."

Aisaka's voice became softer and the rubberneckers shifted, trying to hear.

"...I forgot to tell you, but..."

Ryuuji raised his face, listening to Aisaka's soft voice. Aisaka continued to mutter to him in a voice only Ryuuji could hear. Every ear in the class was pointed in their direction.

"...Can't go home tonight..."

The person directly behind Ryuuji's seat startled, going completely tense upon overhearing those words. *What, what did you just say?* He had a barrage of questions that he couldn't voice, so he wrote down what he had heard. *She said she can't go home tonight*, the note said.

Leaving his dumbfounded classmates in the lurch, Ryuuji continued on with the conversation.

"...Staying over?"

"...Yeah..."

"Then...already prepared..."

"...Yeah..."

The surreptitious commotion propagated throughout the class.

"No way, no way, *no way*! Are they serious?"

"Wait, just now—they couldn't have... Could they...by staying over...? By prepared, they can't mean...!"

"In other words, that means the Palmtop Tiger is sleeping at Ryuuji's house?" the long-haired Haruta-kun gulped, speaking in a small voice.

Turning to Haruta-kun, Noto-kun, in his black framed glasses, lowered his voice. "By prepared...they mean, in other words...like, they're gonna *do it*?! U-uh...th-that's pretty kinky, dude...!"

One of the girls murmured a sound of surprise. "It's officially the first time for anyone in the class," she said.

However, Kihara Mayu stubbornly insisted, "I don't think it's the first!" as her face turned red.

One of the boys looked pained. "I always thought the Palmtop Tiger was kind of cute... I was praying she wouldn't become anyone else's..."

After he said that, a new piece of testimony arose from elsewhere in the room. "I even confessed my love to her last year, but... when I did, she didn't hesitate to tell me she thought all men should just die..."

Everyone was turned towards Ryuuji and Aisaka, who were still standing there quietly. The scene between the two of them had a certain charm to it, as though they were tying together their futures. Aisaka faced the window, without showing her face to anyone, while Ryuuji was scowling, an expression that hinted at some secret resolve to fight someone—maybe even Aisaka's old man.

"K-Kushieda, it seems like your friend might be in trouble tonight!"

Kushieda Minori was silent.

"Kushieda?"

Even after one of the girls hit her in the back, even when she was elbowed, even after other things were done to her, she kept silent as she watched those two.

Incidentally—it wasn't actually that interesting—what had really happened was this:

"Yesterday, your mom left without eating, right? Well, she gave me a message at the time. She said, 'I forgot to tell you, but I can't go home tonight.' I guess it's a regular's birthday, so they're having a party until morning."

"That's Yasuko for you. Does that mean she's staying over at the shop?"

"Yeah, that's what she said."

"Then, she's really already prepared to listen to that old man at the bar, Inage, grumble all night. The regular is old man Inage, right? He just got divorced last year."

"I think that's what she said. Yeah, she asked how Inage-san was... Ahh, what a boring errand. I wish she wouldn't use me to leave messages about household stuff."

"If you've got a problem with it, then don't come over to eat anymore."

"..."

"I told you not to ignore me!"

It was a normal break time, no different from any other for the second-year class C. Takasu Ryuuji was reading manga at his sun-lit desk, and Aisaka Taiga was bored, emanating her don't-bother-me aura while sucking milk out of a carton.

But there was one girl who had the courage to hit Aisaka from behind.

"Hey, Taiga... Could you perhaps spare a minute?"

It was Kushieda Minori. At long last, she had finally made her move. Every eye in class focused on the Palmtop Tiger and the back of the girl who was with her.

"Why are you suddenly being so formal? Wait, Minorin?"

With an unusually serious look on her face, Minori grabbed Aisaka by the nape of her neck and, just like that, yanked her friend up, forcing her to stand and not once letting go of her petite build.

"I-I can walk without you doing that," Aisaka said. "You'll make me fall over!"

"Just get over here."

The only person in the world who could do something like this to the Palmtop Tiger was Minori. If it had been anyone else, they probably would have been chewed up and killed in three seconds flat. Minori pulled Aisaka (still facing away from her) through the onlookers as they all held their breaths. She was pulling the Palmtop Tiger behind her like somebody wheeling luggage.

"...You're coming, too," Minori said.

"Huh...? M-me?"

The one she had designated bluntly with a pointed finger was none other than Takasu Ryuuji. Despite her terseness, and though it was impossible to tell at a casual glance, he might have indulged in a secret smile. After all, even if Minori was making a scene, even if it had just been with a "you," she had still talked to him.

The situation had grown tense on the rooftop—it wasn't obvious, but it definitely had.

The weather was calm and clear. A peaceful breeze blew across the blue skies overhead. But...

"M-Minorin...?"

"Kushieda...?"

Kushieda Minori had turned her back to Ryuuji and Aisaka after dragging them up here. Now she emanated an unusually foreboding aura. For some reason, she wore her jacket on her shoulders, letting the sleeves blow in the wind. "You sweet birds of youth," she muttered to herself in a low voice.

Ryuuji pitched his voice as low as he could manage. "Hey... what exactly is going on here?" he whispered towards Aisaka's ear, thirty centimeters below him.

"Beats me... It's the first time I've ever seen Minorin make a face like that. I wonder if she's mad about something..."

Aisaka's face was also a bit cloudy, just then. She tilted her head uneasily. However, she soon made up her mind and took a step forward.

"H-hey...um, Minorin."

It happened the moment she reached out her hand. Abruptly, sound seemed to stop. It felt as though the world had ceased to function. At the moment she turned, Minori's eyes both glimmered, and right in front of Aisaka, she suddenly leaped up.

"Uh?!" Aisaka exclaimed. She instantaneously protected her face with crossed arms. "What the—?"

With a loud thud, Minori leaped past Aisaka, who stood on guard.

"Takasu-kuuuuuun!"

"Whoa!"

She was right in front of Ryuuji's eyes, just a few centimeters away. She had forcefully slid across the ground, jumped up, then prostrated herself magnificently before him. Her skirt and jacket fluttered in the dust that rose from the concrete.

"I entrust Taiga to youuuuuu!"

It was a scream that could break through the heavens.

"...Wha? Uh? Whaaa?!" Ryuuji stood paralyzed. Minori lowered her head, until the top of it touched the ground before him. Aisaka froze, too. Her jaw stayed dropped as Minori spoke.

"Takasu-kun, this girl...Taiga is an incredibly important close friend of mine! Sometimes she's moody, but she's really a kind girl! Please, please make her happy!"

With loud sobs, Minori embraced Aisaka from afar—she hugged her with her gaze. They remained like that for one second...ten seconds...thirty seconds...

The first one to come back to himself was Ryuuji.

"Kushieda, w-wait, wait—about that, what does that—?"

"Please, stop!"

Minori's face suddenly grew serious. She raised her head and fixed an uncomfortable stare on Ryuuji.

"Please, you can end the charade! Please, Takasu-kun! There's

no need to keep acting. I compleeeetely understand what's going on here. I'm on your side!"

Minori's eyes were serene; she spoke in a resolute voice. As she stared straight into Ryuuji's eyes, she cornered him with an almost violent purity.

"Did you think I hadn't noticed? You're both coming to school together every day, aren't you? I always feel like such a third wheel, and I was waiting for the day you'd open up to me about your relationship...but! No matter how much time passed, you didn't say anything to me! So that's why we're here!"

"No, no, no, no, no way! That, that was—Kushieda, that's wro—"

"I wanted to tell you both—you don't need to sneak around anymore, Takasu-kun, Taiga! I know that you two are dating! I've been wanting to say that for sooooo long!"

While still prostrating herself on the ground, Minori pointed bluntly at Ryuuji. Then, veins burst out on her temple. With a smile like the sun, she gave him a knowing nod.

"No matter what, no matter *what*, you're the person Taiga was meant to be with, Takasu-kun! I won't forgive anyone who interferes with destiny! So please, don't worry about anything and keep on dating! Okay?!"

Don't just say 'okay'! Like he just took a hit to the knee, Ryuuji lost his strength and collapsed on the spot. In that moment, his soul left his body.

He was so shocked he couldn't even open his mouth. His

CHAPTER 5

voice wouldn't work. Even though he wanted to deny it. Even though he *needed* to—

"Y-you're completely wrong! Minorin, you've totally got the wrong idea! We're not in a relationship like that! Just listen to me. Let me explain. Stand up!"

Aisaka was the one making a frantic appeal to Minori as she sidestepped in front of Ryuuji, who was suddenly moved to tears. *That's right, Aisaka. I've become useless, but you can still fix this misunderstanding in my place.* He cheered her on silently, still collapsed on the concrete floor.

But...

"Hee hee hee, no need to be so coy. Congratulations to the new couple!" With flamboyant grace, Minori stood up and beat her skirt. As she did that, she looked at Ryuuji quietly over Aisaka's shoulder.

"...Takasu-kun. If you make Taiga cry...I won't ever forgive you."

For a moment, she looked serious.

Now wait a second! That's not how it is. That's really not how it is. Gasping, Ryuuji frantically tried to squeeze out some words. He reached his hand out and tried to give the retreating Minori an explanation. But his throat. His hands. It was as if he'd been paralyzed from the shock, and his body wouldn't listen to him.

Then, while Ryuuji remained powerless, he saw Aisaka—his last hope for explaining what had happened—killed with the stroke of a sword right before his very eyes. In Ryuuji's vision, the life departed from her small body, as though it were being torn out from behind. Just like that, she stopped moving. The spray of blood dyed Aisaka's whole body red.

"So, that's how it was..." a new voice said. "I thought you two had been together a lot lately. Takasu, I needed you for something and came up here, but...we don't need to worry about that anymore. Congratulations! But that was kind of cold, man! Why didn't you tell me about something so big?"

Kitamura had been there the entire time.

He was standing at the door. He'd seen the whole thing. He'd heard Minori's speech. He had all the wrong ideas.

Then he approached the tiny corpse and dealt the final blow.

"Aisaka. Please take care of Takasu. Please love him for all the many years to come. Now that I think about it, for some reason you two seem like you belong together."

The quiet corpses—one large and one small—remained there, unable to get up.

"Um, sir. Your order...?"

"..."

"..."

"...M-ma'am. Would you like to order something...?"

"...One soda..."

"...The same for me..."

"...Two fountain drinks coming up. The cups are over there."

After that last exchange, the waitress left, but there was no one there to rise and get drinks—just two lifeless bodies.

It was around ten at night, in a family restaurant along the highway, at window seats in the non-smoking section. It was there that the pair of corpses lingered...

Even though it was still April, the larger one wore a loose t-shirt stretched out at the neck. It even had a hairband on—the type that people wore to keep the hair out of their eyes when they washed their face. The smaller one had messy long hair and wore a red checked shirt, its skirt a matching checkered green.

The two of them were worn out. Complete messes. Neither said a word. They hardly even blinked. They were idle, just letting time flow by.

"Why...did it...come to this...?"

The first to speak was the larger corpse, Ryuuji. He put his elbows on the table and held his head. As though speaking to himself, he lowered his voice and muttered, "Wh-where...did we go wrong...? How could Kushieda Minori get such a wrong impression...?"

An aspect of Minori that Ryuuji never knew about had—to his great joy, no matter the circumstance—come to light that day: she was stubborn and wouldn't listen to others. Put another way, she was completely headstrong. Although, given that she was best friends with Aisaka, perhaps it should have been expected that she'd have some idiosyncrasies.

"On top of everything...Kushieda misinterpreting stuff like that..."

To think that his unrequited love interest of nearly one year would jump and prostrate herself before him like that. But, Aisaka, too, who was sitting across from him, had been wounded in the same way.

"..."

Looking like her soul had been completely ripped from her body, Aisaka's empty gaze roamed. She sat on the edge of the sofa chair and stared upwards. Even now, she seemed as though her butt might slip down and send her falling to the floor. *Was this the Palmtop Tiger? Was this the tiger who could knock out a guy with a look, who released her raw power in classroom 2-C?* It pained Ryuuji overwhelmingly.

"A-Aisaka...come on. Get ahold of yourself."

He reached out over the table and shook her small shoulder.

"..."

But Aisaka's soul wouldn't return.

"Aisaka..."

It took up the last of his strength. Ryuuji laid his head down, limp on the table. *Really...what have we come to?*

He should have been used to getting hurt.

He should have been used to being misunderstood. People had mistakenly imagined him to be something he wasn't ever since kindergarten.

"...Oh, right."

Ryuuji came to a realization. It wasn't being misunderstood that had given him such a terrible shock. Minori had cheered him on so seriously with a broad smile on her face. He knew now that he didn't have a hope in hell with her and that was what really got to him.

You're an idiot, he told himself. *That was already so obvious.* It should have been crystal clear that she wouldn't take any particular interest in him—and on top of that, he hadn't done anything to make her like him. What had he been doing getting his hopes up, anyway? Really, he probably didn't even have the right to be depressed.

He stayed in that position for several more minutes, then finally raised his face when he noticed a faint presence.

"Oh..."

Tunk, tunk. He heard two hard sounds.

"...Here. I didn't know what you wanted, so...this is acerola juice with vitamin C."

Aisaka had quietly risen from her seat and brought back bright red drinks for the two of them. She placed the glasses on the table in a line, then slid back down onto the padded seat.

"...Aisaka..."

At some point, life had filled her once again. In front of Ryuuji, Aisaka took in one deep breath, then stretched her back straight and raised her face.

"Sorry. Because we've been together so much—something that *I* insisted on—it's come to this. It's all my fault. Even though I called you a mutt, I failed you as an owner..."

As she muttered, her eyes looked as ill-natured as usual, but she seemed spent. The light that burned in her eyes seemed empty.

A heavy lump had formed in Ryuuji's stomach, and now, it dropped.

Being not-quite together like this was the reason they'd been misunderstood, and Aisaka had been hurt in the same way. In the end, they had both invited this upon themselves. Just like this, by facing each other and always being together.

But...

"...I... doing stuff like this... It's not that..."

He tried saying something, but stopped. Aisaka was hurt in the same way he was. Because of that, he felt he couldn't be selfish with his emotions. He couldn't ask her to confirm that their relationship had caused a misunderstanding. Aisaka opened her mouth in his stead.

"I've...decided..."

She started playing with the ice in her juice with her straw, but she abandoned that and raised her head to look at Ryuuji face to face.

"...I'm going to. Confess. To Kitamura-kun. I'm going to lay it out straight, so there's no room to screw it up... Just a normal, straightforward declaration of love."

Even though her eyes shook with anxiety, she once again added, "I've decided."

Ryuuji sucked in a parched breath. "...Aisaka...why're you suddenly...? No, really, it doesn't matter what you do..."

"That's right. It doesn't matter. And..." She trailed off and said to herself, hoarsely, "If we leave the misunderstanding like this, even you..." Then she spoke audibly again, saying, "...And then we'll end it."

"End it," Ryuuji echoed

"We'll end whatever this is," she said definitively.

After making that declaration, Aisaka's gaze became distant. As though she had sunk into water, the outline of her features abruptly became blurry. Ryuuji was speechless.

"After today, I'm setting you free," she went on. "And then... you can do whatever you want. I won't do anything to stop you. Whether you confess your love to Minorin, or whatever else. No matter what happens after tomorrow's confessions, you don't need to follow me around anymore."

"..."

"As of now, your service as a dog is over. Starting tomorrow... let's go back to how things were before the love letter incident."

A declaration of emancipation.

You don't need to follow me anymore.

That should have been a moment of happiness.

But, really, he still felt speechless.

He wasn't resentful of the way she'd acted until now, he wasn't thankful—he just wasn't anything. There was just one thing, though. That's right—he just wanted to tell her, *Don't be lonely.* But Ryuuji couldn't get the words out of his throat. Even though he'd held the cold glass so long that the tips of his fingers prickled in pain, even though his fingers were getting so cold they were nearly freezing.

However, at some point, Aisaka started smiling. Without making a sound, she smiled. She looked at Ryuuji, but also averted her gaze, slightly awkwardly, as she covered her mouth with both hands and looked down.

"...It's funny. Why've we even been together so much? Even today, we didn't have any plans, but we still naturally got together, like zombies... It's funny. We've been eating together every day, hanging around doing nothing all this time, and getting into fights..."

A moment passed and then a faint laugh leaked out from between those small hands. Her large eyes were thin like the shape of a new moon—Aisaka was really laughing. It was the first time Ryuuji had seen her smile directed at him.

"I didn't want to go home to that big, empty apartment all alone," she said. "So, I kept forcing myself into your house and even made you feed me. Really, I was... Yeah, I was really..."

Hesitating, Aisaka became quiet, and shrugged. Thinking about something, she let her gaze slowly drift away. She quietly shut her thin eyelids. In those eyes, she was closing away something important, something that he'd never seen before—softly, softly, without a sound.

"I really—ha ha, I wonder how to put this. It's just...yeah, that's right. I was lucky I didn't starve. That's right, I really am a klutz. I live by myself in that condo, right?"

She probably wasn't looking at Ryuuji's expression of agreement.

"There's a terrible story, there," she went on. "I never got along with my parents and always fought with them. One time I said, 'I'd rather live anywhere else but here,' and then they really did just conveniently deposit me in that condo. Before I realized it, I was moving out...but it was too late to back down. So then, once I'd moved, I had no idea how to do any chores... I was in trouble. Real trouble. And no one—no one—came to check up on me, either. And my parents knew I was a klutz better than anyone, but I still left home, out of sheer stubbornness. It's stupid, right? I'm a klutz, right? Go ahead and laugh; I won't get angry."

Aisaka's eyes opened.

After she had said all of that at once, he saw all the strength leave her shoulders.

What kind of story is that? Ryuuji wanted to ask, but he held back the groan at the back of his throat. *Because—that's right, isn't it? It really is something that would make you think,* What kind of story is that? *Right?* Because the strange, brief story Aisaka just told was merely the sad tale of an abandoned child. Because those could only be the words of a doll that had been left behind by the king's household, to live alone in the castle.

But Aisaka was laughing. It seemed like she wanted Ryuuji to laugh out loud, too. So...

"Ha...ha ha. Ha ha ha, ha ha ha ha! You really are a klutz..."

"Right."

He laughed. He felt like his heart was being torn to pieces, but with her, he laughed merrily, kindly. Never once before had he wanted to laugh at something so much.

Today was it. Starting tomorrow, it would be like before. Like before—where they didn't even exchange greetings. Just the Palmtop Tiger no one dared to go near and another fearful classmate.

If that were the case, tonight he would laugh as hard as he could. In this shabby restaurant, he'd do it and savor the sight of Aisaka's final smile.

And then, because of that, he showed it to her. He thought she would get a kick out of it.

"Hah, all right," he said. "I'll show you something good. Do you know who this is?"

It was an old picture he always carried around in his wallet.

"Huh? Oh...is that...your dad?!"

"Yeah, you got it."

She blew a huge raspberry and then she laughed. "Aha ha ha ha ha ha ha!" She laughed so much that she got cold stares from the other patrons sitting nearby.

"Wh-what is this! A spitting image! Aha ha, it's great!" Her sides were splitting.

"Look at his eyes. Two peas in a pod, right—me and this old delinquent."

"I can't—c'mon, put it away! Aha ha ha ha ha ha ha!"

Contorting her body, crying, Aisaka laughed until she fell over onto the table. *Bam, bam,* she hit the tabletop, becoming even more of a public nuisance, flailing her feet around. Even when her voice turned hoarse, she kept laughing. It seemed that, using the dread-zilla DNA he'd so thoroughly inherited, he had pushed some button in Aisaka. They were genes he had bemoaned and begrudged, and he was more than a little bitter about them, but if they made her this happy, then there was at least some merit to the inheritance.

"...I've never shown anyone this picture."

"Hah, oh boy, it hurts! I've never laughed this hard in my life! Your family's got weird genes!"

"It's funny, right?"

"It's *too* funny! All right, then. In return for seeing one of your secrets, I'll show you something good—I'll tell you my secret, too," she said and lowered her voice. "Okay, right..." She pursed her lips, trying not to laugh. Her glowingly rosy cheeks puffed up, and her eyes twinkled with mischief. She beckoned him in, and he brought his ear close to those lips.

"...They were salty, right? Those cookies."

"What?!" At the whisper, Ryuuji raised his voice. How—why did she know about how those cookies tasted?

"Gah ha ha! You see, as soon as I got them back, I was so frustrated that I ate one! And it was the *worst*! But you didn't even give me a chance to stop you before you ate them—and you even lied—"

Suddenly, she stopped, right in the middle of her sentence.

She held her breath. Her smile faded. It seemed as though she were searching for the words she'd lost. Then she took one breath. She turned her face down. She hid it from him.

"You're... Ryuuji, as far as dogs go, you're just a mutt. But as a person, you're...okay. So...because of that, because I get that, now, I'm going to stop. You're not worthless. You're really... How should I say this? You shouldn't be a servant, but I think...someone to stand with, shoulder to shoulder..."

She paused, then said, "I don't know what I'm saying."

And just like that, she unexpectedly cut herself off. The next time she raised her face, she wore her customarily cool expression.

"Got my appetite back," she said, as she opened the menu. Ryuuji followed suit. They ordered two Hamburg steaks. They complained about how the Hamburg steaks he'd made earlier were better, which was obvious, and they fought about who would go get the fountain drinks until Ryuuji got kicked out of his seat and was forced to do it. And then, the passing time piled up, hour by hour.

Neither one faltered, and neither one stood higher than the other.

After paying the check, they both started walking home in the middle of the night.

The autumn night was strangely warm, and the crosswind was like something from a dream. It seemed to tickle Ryuuji's skin until he couldn't stand being silent anymore. As though she were drunk, Aisaka also seemed oddly talkative.

They walked along the road for nearly twenty minutes, Aisaka complaining about how her real mother was in another prefecture and how her terrible stepmother was another reason why she had been thrown out of her home.

Ryuuji talked about living alone with his mother and about how he was poor and how people acted like he was stupid and how Yasuko's stalker was a creeper. He talked about how he was misunderstood because of his eyes and about how they continued to make the days of his adolescence humiliating.

That was a wound Ryuuji had never shown anyone. Aisaka, too, had probably shown him wounds she had never shown anyone else. He had enough tact not to ask her, but he was pretty sure that was the case.

And, just then, he was actually really happy. This time passing by was precious.

But, no one could stop time, and slowly, it did pass, until eventually, they found themselves below a corner streetlight ...

"Oh, I can't stand it!" Aisaka vented her anger at the unfortunate, unspeaking electrical pole with an explosive kick. *Whack, thump*—she acted exactly like a drunk as she released one violent kick after another.

"I just hate it...! I swear, the world's *built* to be cold to kids like us! Why doesn't anyone understand that we're dealing with all these things, that we're worrying about all this stuff?!"

She practically choked out those words in frustration. They echoed around the neighborhood in the dead of night. Because of that, Ryuuji didn't stop her; he stayed by Aisaka's side, nodding and agreeing with her.

"Seriously. That's right! Normal people just can't imagine that those of us stuck with sulky-looking faces like you and me get overwhelmed sometimes, just the same as them!"

"Yeah, it makes me angry—angry! Angry, angry, angry!"

Her practiced kicks hit in succession. Suddenly Aisaka turned around, her shoulders heaving with her breath.

"Hey, Ryuuji... Do you think about Minorin and come up clueless, too? Do you agonize over why it never seems to work out and wonder how you could get her to date you?"

"Yeah. I think so."

After answering, he thought about it. Now that she said it, for a while now, ever since he started spending each turbulent day with Aisaka, he felt more distant from those sentimental feelings...

"Then Ryuuji...do you ever cry, too?"

"...Do *you* cry?"

"I do."

She opened herself up. And then there was a moment of silence.

Aisaka slowly looked up at the night sky and tore herself away from the pole. She swept up her disorderly hair so that he could see the white profile of her brittle-looking face.

"Today, I wondered if he thought that I was weird, and whether I might get closer to him, and whether he has a girlfriend and...lots of other things. I thought about all kinds of stupid stuff all by myself... I'm sure no one else knows I do all of that, but... when it comes to me, no one..."

The next word tapered off, so quiet that Ryuuji couldn't hear it completely. Only the echo of her lonely voice passing surreptitiously through the thin clouds of the night sky.

"...Yeah, if anyone knew about that side of you, they'd probably be surprised," Ryuuji whispered, as he too looked up into the darkness and searched for the invisible moon. "No one would think you'd cry like that... I'm the only one who knows."

"Aren't you audacious," Aisaka said. She took a breath, and her gaze shook. "I could say the same thing about you, Ryuuji. I think there are a lot of things only I know."

"What do you mean...? Like what?"

"Even though you've got a... a face like that, you're the type of guy who can barely even talk to the girl he likes. You're the type of guy who can't actually get mad at anyone or hurt anyone. You're the type of guy who can cook, who can clean perfectly... You've got eyes so scary that it makes people afraid to come near you, but you're actually more conscientious than anyone... I'm right, aren't I?"

"Do I really come off that pitiful?"

"...I wouldn't say you're pitiful. It's more that you're..."

Aisaka turned around. Her hair drifted around her like lace in the breeze of the gentle autumn night. She put up a slim finger and said in a faint, quiet voice, "You're a kind person."

"Aisaka..."

So that means I'm just a boring "nice guy," he wanted to retort, but he couldn't put it into words because he saw pain somewhere in Aisaka's expression.

TORADORA!

"I'm the complete opposite of you, aren't I?" she said. "I'm no good. I can't be kind. Because there's so many things I just can't forgive... No, in this world, there's really only a few things I can tolerate. What I see in front of me, everything, all of it, all of them, everyone..."

Her skirt lightly turned up. Her white leg extended out magnificently, cutting through the wind.

"MAKES...ME...ANGRY!"

She landed a deadly high kick on the serene pole. Ryuuji was so shocked by the sudden explosion of emotion that he couldn't speak. He took a big step back, exclaiming to himself in surprise. He could only watch the tiger go berserk.

"It makes me angry, it makes me angry, it makes me *so* angry! Palmtop Tiger, my ass! Everything is NOT completely fine! Why doesn't anyone understaaaaaannd?!"

As though called by the tiger's roar, the golden moon appeared above the two of them.

Aisaka's shadow stretched across the cold asphalt towards the half-dead pole. Ryuuji was just watching, but his shadow also stretched, closing the distance between them.

Their two shadows overlapped, but their bodies didn't touch.

"Everyone, all of it, makes me *furious*! Stupid Minorin... Why wouldn't she listen to me?! Kitamura-kun is the same—why did he just swallow whatever Minorin said?! Why won't he understand?! Minorin and Kitamura-kun both, everyone...every single person, even my mom and dad, all of them, I'll never forgive *any* of them! Because they don't even *try* to understand...! No one *ever* understands!"

Aisaka's voice choked as she took the pole in both hands and kneed it hard. There were probably nights when she worked herself up so much she wanted to cry. On the verge of feverish tears, her breath wavered in frustration, then...

"U-ugh...!"

"Whoa! You idiot, stop!"

She turned around and, with all her strength, headbutted the pole—or at least, she nearly did. Ryuuji dashed forward and put out the palm of his hand, stopping her forehead right before she put herself in danger. Even her forehead wouldn't win against a pole.

"But I'm so *aaannngry*!" she yelled. Then she burst into tears.

Next to him, like a child, Aisaka kept on crying into the autumn night. There was nothing to be done. Ryuuji made a gut decision. But, still, it wasn't like anything he could do would amount to much. It was just better than telling her, *I understand*, and sounding completely shallow.

"...I've got your back," he declared and sucked air into his lungs. Then he shouted in one breath, "I'm aaaanngrrryyyy!"

Although he was unaccustomed to it, he threw in a kick, too, and then a roundhouse. He imagined the K-1 kickboxing he'd seen on TV as he precariously balanced himself.

And just like that, Ryuuji and Aisaka (somewhat unfairly) attacked the pole together. Ryuuji had his own enemies. He felt like a rock placed against the flow of life. Aisaka had enemies, too—at least, he thought she did. She must have had a similar obstacle in her life, embodied by something or other, he thought. That enemy was the feeling of liking someone. It would only get heavier when the time came that she wanted to marry someone. It could probably even be called a psychological complex. Or maybe calling it destiny, or nature, or nurture, or something like that, would be more fitting. Or maybe it was being aware of your own adolescence, of your own helplessness—there were probably a lot of ways to think about it.

But anyway, whatever it was, it didn't have a physical form you could punch or kick, and she'd probably have to keep fighting with it for a long, loooong time. If she didn't kick the pole like this, she wouldn't be able to get it out of her until she died. It would have been better if it had been a wall or a futon, though... *Sorry, pole, you were just unlucky.*

That was why he was doing this. Even though it was foolish and stupid, even if the pole didn't fall down, in the autumn night, they became howling beasts.

Aisaka's enemy was a lot bigger than his and seemed a lot heavier. Ryuuji had that thought while watching the back of her head from beside her. *I get it. In order to stand against that invisible enemy, you became a tiger,* he thought. Her foe was much bigger than a pole, much heavier, and far harder, far more difficult to take down. Aisaka had always wanted the strength to fight against that enemy. That was why she had to become a tiger.

It was a strange thing that Ryuuji and Aisaka's short lives—short in their own ways—had overlapped. Because of that, Ryuuji thought maybe he understood Aisaka. He just couldn't leave her alone with her terribly tired face and horribly hungry stomach.

Even though she was a nuisance, even though she was frustrating, he wasn't sure he would be able to abandon her even if he tried.

And to Ryuuji, that wasn't anything to be unhappy about at all. In fact—

"Ryuuji, stand back!"

"What're you suddenly saying that fo—whoa!"

When he saw Aisaka suddenly raise her face, his thoughts turned to mist and dissipated, out of sheer surprise.

Aisaka was laughing. It was a horrible laugh. Her eyes sparkled atrociously, glinting barbarically with every blink. She attacked her prey with the pure strength of the Palmtop Tiger, crying, "I'll kill you!"

She went to the start of the street and gave herself a lot of space. Then, she pulled up her skirt.

"Just you wait, Kitamuraaaaa! I'm going to confess to youuuuuuuuuu!"

The single member of her audience (Ryuuji) breathed in through his teeth. It was a gruesome approach. Her timing was perfect, and her steps strong. Her short body lithely jumped, and she soared in mid-air. The moonlight reflected in her eyes. Then, her right leg cleaved through the air, and she howled, headed straight towards the pole.

"...Tsk."

At that over-the-top scene, Ryuuji had closed his eyes without thinking. There was an awkward thump, and finally he opened his eyes in panic. He ran over to Aisaka, who was on her butt at the base of the pole.

"Y-you idiot! You, your foot..."

"...Ryuuji. Behold."

"Huh?"

Aisaka pointed to the pole that reached towards the heavens. *What about it?* Ryuuji returned her gaze questioningly as she gave him a broad smirk.

"Don't you think it's a little crooked?"

"What?! No way, it couldn't be! No matter how much a person kicked it, it wouldn't—"

Comparing it to the brick wall behind it, Ryuuji breathed in sharply. "It *is* crooked!"

"See?!"

Victorious, Aisaka laughed. Of course, the pole might have been crooked from the start, or the wall behind it might have been leaning over. Those explanations were more likely than Aisaka's idea that she'd made the pole crooked with one of her kicks.

But Ryuuji believed in her.

He believed that Aisaka, the Palmtop Tiger, had kicked the pole and made it crooked.

Because Aisaka was smiling.

Then Ryuuji glimpsed something in the distance. "...Uh-oh, we're in trouble. Is that a cop?" he said.

They must have made too much of a disturbance—a bicycle was approaching from the other side of the street, and the person riding it was in fact wearing a police uniform. Ryuuji turned to Aisaka, flustered.

"This is bad. We'd better scram! Oh...what now?! What's wrong with you?!"

He found himself with a grimacing klutz, still sitting on the ground.

"O-owww..."

"What?!"

Aisaka, who had until now battled the pole with vigor, sat on the ground with her skirt hem strewn around her. She was rubbing at her right shin. Then with a pitiful expression, she looked up at Ryuuji.

"I might have hit it wrong...It hurts."

He pursed his lips into a thin line. *Oh no!* Ryuuji scratched his head.

"Of course, you would! Jeez...this will probably swell..."

He crouched down and unintentionally scowled. In the dim of the streetlight, he could see that part of the skin just above her thin ankle was horribly bruised.

"Poles sure are hard, huh...? Ow, this hurts a ton..."

"Of course, they're hard! You..."

Ryuuji took in a deep breath. There was only one thing to do.

He crouched down by Aisaka and turned his back towards her. This was what they called chivalry. Even he had some.

"Get on. Really, sometimes, y—ugh! Urgh!"

He had expected her to timidly climb up, but this was the Palmtop Tiger, after all. Even though she said her leg hurt, she swung onto Ryuuji's back with a strong hop. She clutched at his neck so hard he felt like he might die.

"I-It hurts...!" He frantically smacked Aisaka's arms, which were crushing his windpipe and pushing on his arteries. He was trying to convey just how big a crisis she'd put him in.

"Oh no, Ryuuji! Isn't that a policeman? Hurry, you've got to run!"

I just told you that! he thought. With his neck cut off, he couldn't speak, but he nonetheless started running in a hurry.

It was a more roundabout route, but he went down a deserted side road. He tried to soften his footsteps but still ran for his life through the nighttime streets. He slipped into a dark alley bereft of streetlamps. In the strange quiet, they were both at a loss for words, but with the reassuring heat of each other's bodies, they at least didn't need to voice the words, *I'm scared.*

Ryuuji held Aisaka firmly to his back as he moved. She gently pushed her chin against his pulsing neck.

They didn't speak any unnecessary words. They just aimed wholeheartedly towards the light of the large road coming up ahead—

"Ow!"

WHAM. He heard a blunt noise and Aisaka's soft exclamation.

"What?! What happened?!"

Without thinking, Ryuuji stopped and craned his neck around to look at Aisaka on his back. They were close enough that he could feel her breath in the darkness as they exchanged glances.

"I-I got hit by...a signboard or something...it got me right in the forehead!"

"What?! Why didn't you avoid it?"

"It came up suddenly, okay! It's pitch black, and it's not like you noticed, either! ...Owww, ughh, I'm so sick of this..."

"Where? Here?"

Ryuuji reached out his hand and felt Aisaka's slightly warm forehead—it was so dark that he couldn't tell how bad it was just by looking.

"...It's not bleeding. I can't feel a bump, either. You'll be fine, yeah, definitely."

"I have the worst luck."

"It wasn't bad luck, you're just a klutz."

On his back, Aisaka snorted in contempt at the correction. Then Ryuuji set off once again. If he made it to the main road, home was just beyond.

"...Honestly, you're lucky you didn't get cut."

A horn sounded from somewhere far off. Because of that, Ryuuji's faint voice might not have reached the person holding on to him from behind.

"It would've been terrible if you had hurt your face, what with confessing tomorrow and all... You really did get lucky."

Aisaka said nothing, which was fine.

He could feel her soft cheek against his neck. She wasn't hurt, and she was safely on his back. It was fine like that. He was fine with just having that.

Keeping an eye out for any sign of the police bike's pursuit, they finally cleared the alleyway. They returned to the broad side-walk of the roadway, brightly lit by streetlights. Every now and then they passed someone on their way home from work, or a middle-aged woman walking her dog. No one spared Ryuuji or Aisaka a glance. Each and every one of them had their own hardships to bear. The salary men and office ladies, the grandmas and grandpas, all of them probably had their own enemies and their own weights. All of them must have had nights when they felt like beating up a pole. But they were adults, so they didn't.

Suddenly, the strange image of passersby locked in a blood-bath with a pole floated through Ryuuji's mind, and he chuckled without thinking.

Aisaka noticed. "What are you laughing at?" She contorted and bent forward. She breathed against the side of Ryuuji's face.

"Nothing... It's not a big deal."

"What?! What is it? Tell me, tell me! Spit it out!"

"Ugh-gug."

His neck was being firmly squeezed.

"Y-you know..."

"I want to know. Hey, what were you laughing about?"

"...It's nowhere close to a big deal, so don't worry about it... I-I can't breathe!"

"If you're not gonna talk, I'll make it so you can't talk at all."

"Guuuhhh!"

All right already—she's really something, Ryuuji thought, flailing about to try and defend his windpipe. She was tyrannical, stubborn—and selfish. She was a despotic tiger who wouldn't let anything go any way but the exact way she wanted. He'd endured a mountain of suffering—that one time, and that other time, and *that* time, too—just from getting involved with her.

He'd had that thought over and over again...and it kept coming back, to the point he figured himself immune to it. He had thought the warm frame clinging to him wouldn't be able to stir any emotions in him at all. He never thought approaching the upper-class condominiums Aisaka lived in would make his heart pound.

But even though he thought that...

The arm around his neck suddenly loosened.

"Here's good," Aisaka whispered, and patted his shoulder once.

In front of the condo's entrance, she hopped off his back. His back was suddenly bare and without weight, and the warmth also disappeared. Losing it all, he turned to look at Aisaka, who stood before the glass door.

And then he felt his heart squeeze painfully—so this was how much it hurt.

"Well, Ryuuji. We're right on time. See?" She put out her slender wrist and pointed at the face of her wristwatch. The two hands on the face pointed right at 11:59.

"Ahh, that was exhausting, right?" she went on. "But we made it home safely. Today's the end of it all. Once the day's over, you won't be my dog anymore. There's thirty seconds left... Hey, don't you have something to say for yourself?"

"...Something to say...? Like what?"

"As a mutt. Don't you have any last words for your owner, Ryuuji?"

"...Uh... Don't you think that's a little sudden...?"

With a distance of two meters between them, Aisaka was thinly smiling. At least, he thought she was. She tilted her small head to the side and seemed to be waiting for Ryuuji's words. But did he even have something to say? Was there *anything* to say?

"...Ten seconds...five seconds..."

He didn't say anything.

The wind that passed through divided them. Aisaka lowered the arm she'd used to show him the watch. Then, she said, "Bye bye."

"Right... T-tomorrow! Good luck tomorrow!"

And that was it.

"Bye bye, Takasu-kun."

HE SLEPT IN.

He thought he had made rice for breakfast and the bento, but he'd forgotten to turn on the rice cooker.

He forgot to give Inko-chan her food and change her water, too.

He left the house in such a hurry that he wore mismatching socks on either foot.

"...There's got to be something wrong with me..." he said to himself in a low, small voice, as he looked at his own feet. The right foot, black. The left foot, navy.

It was when he stood in front of the shoe cubbies at school that he first noticed his regrettable mistake, while changing from loafers to slippers. He couldn't do anything about it now; they stood out strikingly. The colors were completely different. How had he screwed up so badly...?

But he had no time to think about it. He was on the verge of tardiness, and the guidance counselor was standing right there. Rushing students continued to hurry in. Ryuuji hung his head a little and sprang up the stairs to the classroom, hurrying along at a speed that wouldn't get him in trouble. But...he completely missed the last step and hit his shin. Pure agony struck him; he couldn't make a sound. His eyes narrowed in his delirium, accidentally scaring the people passing by below.

He was already out of breath, and as he rubbed his leg, he only thought of one thing. The reason why his life was in such disarray must have been because he had parted ways with Aisaka the day before.

Ryuuji's morning should have been easier, as he hadn't had to go through the trouble of getting her in the morning, or making an extra bento. This morning was supposed to have been the return to his comfortable life. Even so, with all that had happened, it seemed that a life disturbed couldn't so easily recover. *Maybe living as a dog left a stain on me,* he thought pitifully, but the quiet morning without Aisaka's jeers also felt strangely quiet.

He wondered how she was doing. He couldn't help but think about it as he walked at a snail's pace. Had she woken up without him coming to get her? Was she running late? Had she been able to bring a lunch? Not that he was one to speak—today he was eating a convenience store meal, himself...

Thinking about such thoughts wouldn't do him any good,

though, so he shook them away. He threw open the classroom's sliding door and took a step in.

"...Whoa!"

He stumbled, completely taken by surprise. Without thinking, he backed out of the room and closed the door.

What was that?

While he was still alone in the hallway, he took a deep breath in and exhaled. He calmed himself, then thought, *What was that I just saw? How did it get like that?*

He couldn't calm himself down, but he had to check again. Or, really, he couldn't just not go into class. Resolute, he focused on his hand and, calming his heart, he opened the door again.

"...You got that, right?"

This time Ryuuji froze.

What had entered his ear was a low, thoroughly menacing voice. The words were hard, vibrating with the promise that they'd never forgive anyone who disagreed.

"If I hear anything this boring from anyone else, ever again... I'll show them no mercy."

The person making an address at the center of the classroom, with her back to Ryuuji, was Aisaka Taiga. Also known as the Palmtop Tiger.

And the whole class was nearly plastered to the wall, trying to distance themselves from Aisaka as much as possible. Everyone vigorously nodded their heads up and down in frantic agreement.

"What is this?" Those were the words that he got to come out.

He'd say them as many times as he needed to: "What is this?"

"...You're sure you heard me? Don't make me repeat myself!" The small tiger roared one more time.

The quaking boys and girls chorused a pitiful, "Understood!"

When he looked more closely, the desks and chairs around Aisaka were all tumbled over, like they'd been kicked. Bags and people's belongings were scattered around—the classroom was really in a terrible state. It was like a hurricane had blown through. Aisaka's voice had been quiet, but her shoulders heaved violently with her breathing. They went up and down, as though she had just been yelling. Maybe—no, it was *definitely* Aisaka who had done this. But why?

"Oh...Takasu..." Someone noticed him and muttered his name. Yes, he was indeed Takasu...

"Wh-what...? What is it?"

Why did everyone in the class have the same strange expression? He was glad they weren't expressions of disgust, but their faces made him uneasy—they were strained. They were all lined up, all of them wearing an expression he had no words for.

And then, Aisaka turned around without a sound. Her eyes silently met Ryuuji's. Aisaka didn't even say a good morning. Instead, she dropped her chin, and told the people in the class, "Scram."

Everyone who had been trembling together started heading back to their own seats in groups. Several stopped by Ryuuji.

"...T-Takasu...sorry. For spreading weird rumors."

"Huh? Weird rumors?"

"Sorry, we won't do any prying again."

"...Wh-what? What are you talking about?"

He approached Noto, who he was normally friendly with.

"...Hey, Takasu, I didn't mean anything bad by it. I actually thought it was pretty awesome for you and that's it... And I guess I was feeling a little jealous, too. Sorry. I won't ever do it again." Noto spoke meekly, with a strained expression. Ryuuji grabbed Noto's retreating shoulder and, flustered, asked him what he really meant.

"Wait a second. What are you going on about? What the heck happened? This definitely looks like one of Aisaka's rampages. Just what did she do?"

"Well, um..."

"Just tell me already."

Noto's face twitched uneasily, and his eyes nonchalantly wandered to the left. He was among those who weren't scared of scrutiny from Ryuuji's sanpaku eyes, which were now pressing him for an answer. But Ryuuji didn't move to let go of Noto's shoulder. He didn't intend to, not until he knew the reason. Maybe understanding that, Noto said, "Let's see, how can I phrase this..."

He told Ryuuji the gist of what had happened. "Uum... It looks like she found out that...we were gossiping about you and the Palmtop Tiger."

"Gossiping?"

"Uhh...yeah, like that you two were maybe dating and stuff. And then the Palmtop Tiger got all fired up and put an end to it.

She was like, 'Takasu-kun and I aren't involved with each other at all,' and then she turned into a monster... I was terrified... This was, like, the first time I ever saw the Palmtop really show her stuff. I'm never gonna mess with her. Then she said, 'Don't say anything stupid. Don't just spit out whatever comes into your heads. If anyone spreads any more gossip like this, I'll kill them. I'll really kill them, in the nastiest way you can think of—got that?!' And Kushieda tried stopping her, and that was a complete bust, yeah? Right, Kushieda?"

The one Noto had called out to was Kushieda Minori, who had just been passing by—she was the one and only person who should have understood the Palmtop Tiger. But the sun-like smile that she always had was missing.

"Oh...right, Takasu-kun. Ummm, I wanted to..."

With a quiet gaze, as though she were thinking about something deeply, she searched the depths of Ryuuji's eyes. She was trying to say something. But...

"...Minorin. Don't say anything uncalled for. I *will* get angry, even if it's you," Aisaka said, grilling her from behind with a hard voice. "I want you to speak to Takasu-kun—tell him that you understand that what happened yesterday was a misunderstanding. Say it out loud. Honestly, I don't care about what anyone else in the class thinks. The one opinion that matters is yours, Minorin."

"...Taiga."

"Say it, Minorin," Aisaka commanded vehemently, like a child, her lips formed into a line. Without removing her eyes from Minori, never once looking at Ryuuji, she furrowed her brow intensely.

For a while, Minori silently took in that stare. Then, as though she had been worn down, she said, "I got it," and once again turned to face Ryuuji.

"Takasu-kun. Sorry for the misunderstanding yesterday."

"Ah, it's okay! That... that's not something you need to apologize for..."

"Taiga told me to."

Ryuuji's secret crush had a slightly bewildered look in her eyes. Even as she faced him, she looked like she didn't really believe what she was saying.

"...Taiga really wanted me to say that. I'm supposed to tell you it's all a misunderstanding. But...the only reason Taiga would go this far is..."

Her mouth formed the word *probably*—but then at the same moment, something disturbed the precarious balance.

"Whoa! What is this mess?! Does morality just fall by the wayside when the class representative is late?"

Kitamura had arrived at school and was making a fuss. Minori shut her open mouth and cut off what she was going to say. She pivoted her heels, so that her back faced Ryuuji, and patted Aisaka's head.

"Don't make that face," she said in her usual airheaded voice and headed straight to her seat.

Then, at the clueless Kitamura's direction, they started cleaning up the overturned desks and chairs.

"Hurry up, hurry up! If Koigakubo-sensei sees it like this, the shock would make her even more of a spinster than she already is!"

Ryuuji watched as Aisaka stepped toward Kitamura, right in front of him. Then, standing on her tiptoes, at a volume only Kitamura could hear, she whispered something.

Kitamura's expression looked mysterious for a moment, but he immediately nodded at Aisaka with his usual carefree expression.

In Ryuuji's eyes, Aisaka's lips seemed to move, as though saying, "There's something I want to tell you after school."

Without mucking it up, without stuttering from nervousness, without falling over or doing anything wrong, and without help from a certain dog, Aisaka had successfully spoken to Kitamura.

Another day in the second-year class C had ended, though the situation was still pretty tense. In fact, Ryuuji hadn't been able to peel his eyes off of Aisaka and Kitamura.

After the bachelorette (clothed in a fashionable outfit that was soft pink from head-to-toe and totally didn't fit her age) walked off after ending ceremonies, the class went into a commotion all at once. Some people went to clubs, some to their committee meetings, while others asked each other to walk home together. There were also those who stayed behind to keep talking—the ones who signaled to each other with their eyes and left the classroom together.

CHAPTER 6

Unconsciously, Ryuuji kicked the bottom of his own seat, then got up and followed after Aisaka and Kitamura. He took long strides, while still trailing slightly behind them.

It might have been in bad taste, but...that thought only troubled him for a few seconds. *But, but, but,* he kept thinking, doing his best to keep from breaking out into a run, or letting his footsteps make too much noise.

This *was* Aisaka, after all. He didn't know what kind of blunder she might make. She might trip. She might fall down the stairs. She might get nervous and tongue-tied and start crying. Whatever the blunder, he had to go along because Aisaka was a super-epic klutz—and also because he was the only one who knew that truth.

Because of that—because he was worried, because he couldn't take his eyes off her, because...

Because?

"...Tch."

As he followed along behind the two, watching them recede down the stairs, his feet came to a sudden stop.

Ryuuji questioned himself anew.

Because. What did that word mean to him, really? So Aisaka was a klutz, and that worried him, sure. But what he could do about it? Help her? But why?

What kind of relationship did he and Aisaka—no, what *right* did he have to save Aisaka or do anything else? They were pretending everything up until now hadn't happened. Aisaka had said they would return to their relationship from before the love letter happened.

That meant he should have also made himself forget about the Aisaka that only he knew. He ought to think about everything from a more realistic perspective and avoid getting sentimental. Even if she messed up trying to confess her love to the guy she liked, what kind of help could he even give her? Would he jump out in front of her and say, "Don't worry! I'll protect you!"

Man, what was he thinking? It wasn't even funny.

His eyebrows scrunched. His eyes narrowed into a terrible squint, glinting perilously. But he wasn't angry. He wasn't going out to settle a debt or choke somebody he didn't like. It wasn't that... No one would understand, but *he* wasn't like that, either.

"Huh," he breathed out heavily. "...I should go home."

He put his strength into his feet and changed direction. He turned his back to the two of them as they left and returned to the after-school classroom. Although no one noticed, it seemed the back he turned on them had grown by several centimeters over the previous few days.

Noto, as well as Haruta—who had come to speak to him lately—invited him to go somewhere, but he rejected them and went back to his seat. For some reason, he couldn't put himself at ease. He couldn't work up the will to hang out with friends before going home. Yet, he didn't feel like going straight home, either, so he decided to head out on his own and stop by a bookstore.

Once he finished getting ready to leave, he started walking down the hallway to visit the bathroom. He passed by someone who had just finished wiping his hands. They left, leaving Ryuuji alone by himself. The empty bathroom returned to cold silence. Only the fragrance of an especially strong air freshener tickled his nose.

Once he finished, he headed to the sink, washed his hands, and glanced at his face inside the mirror. It wasn't any different from usual—it was still his customary, humorless expression. It wasn't a reflection he would suddenly start admiring. Really, he'd grown tired of it. Because of that...really, no matter what he did...

The focus of Ryuuji's thoughts weren't on his face. He thought about something else entirely. He mulled it over.

"...She made such a ridiculous expression..."

He was thinking about the Palmtop Tiger. Somewhere, right at that moment, she was giving it her all.

That whole day, during class and at their breaks, Ryuuji had obliquely stolen glances to see how Aisaka was doing. With the passage of time, Aisaka's face went through a bewildering evolution of colors. Just earlier in the middle of homeroom, it had looked exactly like a Noh mask. It had gone past red and blue to stark white.

She was going to be confessing, so it would have been better if her face had been cute. She really was such an awkward person.

And speaking of awkward—that morning's commotion. She had rampaged through the classroom, even turning that ferocious expression on Minori. Actually, it was probably exactly *because* it was Minori that she'd used such a grim look.

In other words, Aisaka had caused all that chaos for him—for Ryuuji and his unrequited love for Minori. She had done it so that Minori wouldn't misinterpret his intentions. Aisaka's rampage must have been entirely for that purpose.

Now that he thought of it, Aisaka had never made such a commotion over him before. Which meant she must have done it to fix Kitamura's misunderstanding of her, as well. But Kitamura hadn't been there that morning when Aisaka had been rampaging.

In other words, it had been genuine. For Ryuuji, Aisaka had...

"...Really, now..."

With a sigh, the words escaped him. Awkward, stupid, a klutz...those words couldn't properly convey what she was.

She didn't have to do anything like that. There were better ways she could have gone about it. Instead, she'd used the most disastrous method available. She really was—to a pitiful extent—a kind person. In his heart of hearts, he really believed that. Aisaka was a genuinely kind girl. The word seemed laughably ill-suited for the Palmtop Tiger, but he couldn't help but believe it.

She had told Ryuuji that *he* was kind, and then cried that she couldn't be kind to others—but she was the kindest of girls. You wouldn't know it unless you were by her side, but it was definitely the truth. Maybe it didn't mean much, but it was true for Ryuuji.

"Whoa!"

At the sudden voice, he snapped around. A guy had come

into the bathroom from another class, but froze with a yell on his face when he saw Ryuuji looking at him in surprise.

The guy stepped back and shouted, "Uh, sorry for causing you trouble!!" and left. It seemed he had been startled by the unexpected sharpness of the gaze Ryuuji turned on him. By reputation only, he was still feared on the same level as the Palmtop Tiger.

In the hallway, people were now surely spreading word that Takasu had holed himself up in the bathroom, that it was dangerous to go in. That meant no one would come in for a while. The situation perfectly fit his delicate mood; he didn't want to see anyone.

As obsessed with cleanliness as ever, Ryuuji went into the back to fling open the window, figuring that if no one was coming in for a while, he might as well let in the breeze. Humidity contributed to bad odor, after all.

He turned the latch, opened the window—and then froze.

"Kitamura-kun! Kitamura-kun, I... Kitamura-kun I... Um... Well..."

"...What?!" Ryuuji muttered and held his head, still motionless. *This can't be a hallucination and, uhhh, that means...*

He was hearing Aisaka's voice perfectly, clearly—completely.

The men's restroom was on the second floor, as the restroom on the first floor was for guests. Outside the school building—or rather, between the restroom window and a stand of trees—there was a clearing. Still finding it hard to believe, Ryuuji looked down. His last hopes of being somehow mistaken were crushed.

In that indiscreet location, Aisaka and Kitamura stood together. If they had put even a little thought into it, they would've realized that they could be overheard by anyone using the toilet.

"Of all the places...why would you *ever* choose the place behind the bathrooms...?" Ryuuji said under his breath.

What a klutz.

Still clutching his head, Ryuuji gave a low moan. He slid down to sit beneath the window. The place was deserted, but the reason why...was, frankly, because of the smell.

He crouched underneath the window he'd flung open and buried his head in his knees until he no longer had air to breathe. In the end, Aisaka really was a klutz. First of all, if someone else had come here and opened the window like him—then what would have happened? The sight of the two of them would have most likely been completely out in the open, and there would have been nothing they could do about it.

For that very reason, Ryuuji decided to stay where he was for the time being. If someone came, he would glare horribly at them and make them leave. He'd serve as a guard, just like that.

First, however, he would close the window so that their voices wouldn't reach *his* ears, either. That in mind, he started to get up.

"Wait a second." It was Kitamura.

At the sound of his voice, Ryuuji found himself unable to move.

"I think I more or less understand where this conversation is going. But it'd be fairly embarrassing for everyone if I misunderstood, so before I hear you out, let me confirm one thing... I'll just come straight out and say it. You're dating Takasu, right?"

Ryuuji's heart jumped with a start. He couldn't just go around eavesdropping—no, *eavescrouching*. He knew that, but once he heard his own name, he just couldn't block it from his ears. *No, you can't do this, hurry up and close the window. If not that, then run away...!*

"T-Takasu-kun is..."

He knew he should close the window, but he couldn't move. Aisaka's voice, probably so shrill from nervousness, wrapped itself around Ryuuji's body as though trying to squeeze him.

"Takasu-kun is, is... is, is... is..."

She couldn't get past "is."

You idiot, what are you doing? What are you hesitating for? You have to deny it, don't you—what do you think you're standing around the back of the restrooms for...?! Ryuuji shouted inside his head, still crouched, unable to make a sound, in pure agony. But Aisaka couldn't continue.

The silence just piled on. In the end, she couldn't even say "is" anymore. If Kitamura were a normal guy, this would be the point where the tension got the better of him, and he'd say, "Well, if you've got nothing else to say, I guess we're done here." Even Kitamura—no, actually, Kitamura was much busier than the average guy. Surely, if it continued like this, he would leave. Without knowing what Aisaka's feelings were, Kitamura would leave.

Hurry up and say it. You have to! Ryuuji gripped his hands together hard and gritted his back teeth. He forgot to breathe, yet Aisaka couldn't bring herself to make a sound. The silence seemed like it lasted an eternity, getting heavier and heavier.

It might have been impossible for her from the start. Confessing her love for someone she couldn't even call out to in class might have been a rash plan. That was it, then. Closing his eyes, Ryuuji gave up.

But just as he did, Aisaka said, "What happened with Takasu-kun was just a misunderstanding by Minorin! Kitamura-kun, I..."

The wind blew.

"...I like *you*..."

...*Ah*.

Gradually, the strength left his legs. His butt almost reached the floor, but he saved himself from reaching that dangerous destination.

Ryuuji's breath stopped again. He felt like some sound might escape him, so he kept his lips firmly closed. Eventually, he held his mouth shut with both hands. *You're amazing*. The words surged through his heart, over and over.

Kitamura was someone Aisaka couldn't even talk to and she had been about as nervous as could be—yet she had still confessed. She'd told Kitamura her feelings. Ryuuji didn't think he could ever do something like that. Even if someone told him to confess to Minori in just the same way, he doubted he would have gone through with it. He had cheered Aisaka on irresponsibly,

but what Aisaka was doing right that moment was impossible for him. He could never be that straightforward.

The words continued to vibrate in his chest. Even though Ryuuji wasn't part of the scene that was transpiring, Aisaka's determination and courage pierced through his heart like a light. Surely her feelings had pierced straight through Kitamura's heart, as well. They must have—and then swept him away. It must have transported him somewhere.

Yes, that was how it should be. If he had any heart at all, it must have been moved. Everything was going the way it was supposed to.

Ryuuji felt as though something had been stolen from him, but surely he was mistaken.

"So, you like me," Kitamura said, "and the stuff about Takasu was all a misunderstanding. So, Kushieda's impression of you and Takasu...was just a misconception...?"

"...That's right. No matter what I said, Minorin wouldn't believe me, so..."

As if thinking things over, Kitamura paused. Eventually he seemed to come to an understanding.

"I see. In that case, allow me to apologize. It seems I had completely the wrong idea. Kushieda's really strong-willed, too. I understand. Yes, I understand completely."

"...Yeah."

Kitamura's voice was gentle.

Aisaka's voice, even now, was so hoarse it sounded like it might disappear.

And finally, there was Ryuuji's breathing, as he held his hands to his mouth to keep from making noise.

All three sounds quietly and slowly crossed through the empty men's restroom. Ryuuji's surroundings vibrated with the gentle noise as he crouched there alone, trying to muffle any sound he might make.

He tried to shake off the feeling of vibration that continued to resonate in his chest and breathing. He shook it off and stood up, but as he tried to close the window and go home, Aisaka burst out, saying, "B-b-b-but! But you see!"

Outside the window, her voice was high and jumpy.

"But, it's not like I dislike Takasu-kun!" she said. "He's not that bad at all! When I'm with him, it's easier to breathe! Well, it's always hard for me to breathe, but...even though I thought that...Takasu-kun... Ryuuji always makes me the best fried rice! Whenever I need someone, he's always there for me! Even when I lied to him, he made me feel better! I want to be with him as much as I can! I even wish he were here right now! Without Ryuuji, I almost feel torn, I almost hurt, because Ryuuji...I always, always—even now! Because he would always be there! It's because of him that I can do this now...!"

Dumbfounded, Ryuuji's whole body was frozen.

What are you doing? Just what kind of mess are you making now?

Even now, she sounded like she was about to start crying. What was she doing making pronouncements like that? *Aisaka...*

225

"...I'll never stop liking him, not ever. To me, Ryuuji is... Ryuuji is..."

That's almost like—almost exactly as though—

"I see."

He heard Kitamura's voice, which seemed to have a smile in it.

"That's fine. I think I understand how you feel, Aisaka. Anyway...if the truth is that you've gotten closer to Takasu, that's okay. Honestly, I'm relieved to hear it."

"R... relieved...?"

"Yeah. Do you remember? I confessed to you myself, just about a year ago. I said...you're beautiful, and I like your straightforward personality and the way you don't hide your anger! I dig it!"

No one ever told me anything about that! Ryuuji's eyes opened wide. Astonishment overflowed him as he stood there, but Aisaka said nothing. The only one who was so surprised that his legs turned to jelly was Ryuuji. He was the only one who hadn't known.

"And, well, right after, you turned me down in one second flat."

"...I remember. It's not like I'd forget. I've heard a lot of confessions, but that was definitely the weirdest. Since then, whenever you came to my class to talk to Minorin about club stuff, I always recognized you... I remembered."

"Is that so? You gave me the cold shoulder so hard, I thought you didn't even remember what happened. Back then, I told you how I felt because I thought you were beautiful—but since you've known Takasu, you've grown even more charming. It's like...you're able to put on a funny face, now."

"A-a funny face? Me?"

"That's right. Whenever you're with Takasu, you always make really happy faces. So, I was relieved. Takasu is a really great guy. And Aisaka, I think that the way you think of him really makes you a lovely girl."

It seemed that Kitamura was smiling brightly. And then...

"...Wh-what did I just say?!"

He heard the sound of Aisaka's shout as she realized the mistake she had made.

"Wait, wait a second...what am I saying...? Kitamura-kun, what are *you* saying?! Ryuuji doesn't have anything to do with this, um...what?! My face is funny?! No wait...*what?!* Now hold on a second! Did I tell you that I like you?! Did I actually tell you that?! Uh, but...no way, what's going on here?! I don't like it, I don't like it one bit, what is this?"

On and on she went, becoming more flustered by the moment. Having lost herself, the Palmtop Tiger howled. Anyone other than Kitamura probably would have been in grave danger.

"Aisaka. It's okay. It's fine," he said.

"I-I-I-It's fine?! What's *fine* about this?! I don't even know what I'm saying! What's fine about that?!"

"Thanks for the sentiments, really. I'm really happy. I think from here on, we'll definitely become good friends."

"Fr... fri..."

Still in a state of panic, Aisaka's voice seemed no longer able to form words.

"That's right, friends."

Friends.

That hadn't been the relationship Aisaka had asked for. Naturally, Aisaka should have said, *No, that's not what I meant.*

That's what you should say, Ryuuji thought.

But despite that...

"...Friends... You and I...become..."

But even if she should have said it like that, the fact was, she hadn't. Aisaka couldn't say, *I like you, I want to be your girlfriend, not just your friend. I rejected you once when you confessed, but while I was watching you, I came to like you. I like you now. I want to be your girlfriend.*

She still couldn't say those utterly important words and fix what she'd done.

The Palmtop Tiger, a self-proclaimed queen, withdrew her claws of her own accord. "Yeah." With that one syllable word, she withdrew one step from that place. She had retreated.

"Well then, see you tomorrow!"

Kitamura's cheeriness, at best, was filled with a considerateness that never changed, regardless of his mood. At worst, it was the bright voice of someone who couldn't read the room.

Aisaka recovered from her panic and went back to her normal monotonous way of speaking. "See you tomorrow. Bye."

And so it went.

Ryuuji slapped his forehead in disappointment. He scratched his head and closed his eyes. He could hear from the retreating voices that the two of them had started walking in different directions. He could only groan.

"...She is the *biggest* klutz..."

You didn't get Kitamura to understand.

Just how many tears, smiles, and fears do you have in that heart of yours that Kitamura criticized dead-on? Just how much loneliness, how much of the love you feel for Kitamura—how many frail emotions are you hiding?

And even though it must hurt, just how kind are you? He didn't understand what you were saying. You didn't get him to understand you at all.

He braced his feet, which had gone numb from the cold, and slowly started walking.

After saying goodbye and leaving like that, Aisaka had to be somewhere nearby. She would be walking by herself, wearing an expression that said she was completely fine, while hiding a heart no one else knew. And when she turned her back to Kitamura, Ryuuji knew she must have cried with a voice no one else knew, too. With uncertain steps, while no one was looking, she was letting herself cry. He was certain of that.

And so, if he was the only one who knew, a question remained: What was he, Takasu Ryuuji, to do?

"That's easy," he said.

His response was determined, but he didn't actually know

what he was supposed to do—or at least, his head didn't. His chest knew, though. And his skin did, too. His bones, his muscles, the body that had spent such a long time with Aisaka—it all knew.

Because of that, as long as he left it up to his body to move him—and didn't head in the wrong direction—he would be able to go just where he needed to.

He was certain.

In twilight, like a certain other time they had walked home together...

"...What is it with you?"

Ryuuji, after some running, finally caught up with Aisaka and grabbed her shoulder. It was a lane in a quiet neighborhood with few passersby.

Aisaka turned around and gave him a dubious expression. She glared at him as he panted, out of breath.

"Stop it. You're not my dog anymore, so you don't need to hang around me." Her assertion was cold and blunt as she shook off his hand and tried walking ahead.

"You're close to crying," he said to her back. "You're probably depressed about your failed confession, aren't you? I mean... it wasn't quite a rejection, at least."

"Tsk!" Leaping back to gain some distance, Aisaka shouted, "Y-you were...spying on us?!"

"...I didn't do it on purpose, I'll have you know. It was only because you messed up. Why, of all places, did you make your confession under the men's restroom? I went in there and happened to hear you."

Aisaka's cheeks turned red enough to see under the moonlight. "I-Is that true?!" She spoke falteringly—it seemed, somehow, she really hadn't known.

"Well, what are you going to do? Do you want to go shopping for dinner? Or maybe, in commemoration of your failed confession, we should go to that family restaurant from yesterday again? I'll even listen to your whole sob story—but one day only, got it?"

"...Wait. What? What are you saying?"

Aisaka was petrified as she faced Ryuuji. Her large eyes opened wide, as though faced with something unbelievable.

"Now that I think about it, there's a special on pork today."

"I-I'm not talking about *pork*!"

"So, you want beef?"

"Not the beef, either! It's not that... Why?! What is this?! You're already..."

"Do you really want to cook by yourself?"

"I just told you! I told you... you can stop, already! We're through! We're not doing any of that anymore..."

"I'm staying by your side," he told her clearly. At a loss for words, Aisaka scowled. Still looking at those eyes, Ryuuji said it again. He spelled it out for her.

"I'm by your side. I'll cook your meals. Come over, just like always. I'll make your bento, too, and I'll come get you in the morning. So..."

"Don't say it... don't say that!" Her shriek echoed though the quiet lane. "Do you even understand what you're saying?! If you do stuff like that, people will get the wrong idea all over again! Minorin *still* isn't fully convinced! You really don't care what Minorin thinks of you?!"

"Not really." The words came out of his mouth with surprising ease.

"In that case, next time *I'll* make a scene. I'll throw a fit while Kitamura is around, to clear up any misapprehensions."

"Wh-why are you...?" A tear dripped down her white face.

See, look, Ryuuji thought. *She really was crying in a place no one—except me—would see.*

"What is it, what're you...? Why? Why would you do that?! I told you you're not a dog anymore! So, you don't need to do that anymore!"

"...I don't even know, myself. But I want to do it. Because you'll cry. I can't just leave you on your own. I can't help but worry about whether you're hungry. I'm the compulsively kind Ryuuji-kun, remember?"

"Wh-what's with you?!" Aisaka glared at Ryuuji through her tears, with eyes that had a strong light in them.

"Who asked you to do that?! I'm not a kid, so leave me alone! I don't want you to worry about me or anything!"

"Ohh, is that right?" Ryuuji countered.

Finally, his brain understood what the rest of him already knew.

The reason why he wanted to be by Aisaka's side.

The reason why he couldn't help but worry. Why he couldn't leave her alone.

"And I'm not going to be your dog anymore, all right? I'm going to stand beside you, side by side."

"...What?!"

"A dog can't actually stand by you."

He wasn't a dog. A dog was all wrong.

A dog came when it was called, but a tiger wouldn't call on anyone. It wouldn't ask for help from anyone; it was a tiger. A tiger was just that type of beast.

Because of that, because he was there now, he was no one's dog.

He might laugh, and maybe someone would laugh at him— but despite that, Ryuuji continued. Now, no matter what happened, he wanted to say it. He wanted to tell Aisaka.

"I'm a dragon. You're a tiger. Since forever, the only creature strong enough to stand by a tiger has been the dragon. Because of that, I'll become Ryu—a dragon—and I'll keep on standing by your side."

In order to stand beside the Palmtop Tiger, Takasu Ryuuji would become a dragon. He had decided. Even if he were laughed at, even if she made fun of him—but then...

"...Ai...saka...?"

She wasn't making fun of him. She wasn't even laughing at him.

The girl before him seemed incapable of even making a sound. She was bracing both her legs as she stood, and her cheeks were wet from tears, as she looked straight up at Ryuuji.

She looked like she could be angry. She looked like she could be sad. She looked like she could be frightened or troubled. And, of course, she looked like she could be surprised.

She was stoppering her small body full of emotions. Like a bomb nearly about to go off, she clenched tight one fist.

"...Tai...ga..."

When he said her name, Aisaka's—Taiga's eyelids fluttered, as though she had been flicked.

"Equality is like that, right?" he went on. "You'll call me Ryuuji. So, I'll call you Taiga." Then he said, "That's fine, right?"

That was when it happened.

"What's that supposed to mean?!" she said. The shadow that lengthened from the base of her feet seemed to suddenly build up in size. It must have been a trick of the eyes, but...

"Just how bold can you get?! You think you're good enough to use my first name?! E-equals? Don't make me laugh! What a shameless display! Understand your place, Ryuuji! You idiot!"

"...Uh..."

Yup, the bomb had gone off.

"Hah, you don't even understand the first thing about what you're saying—do you?! If you did, no way could you say things like that! What was that? Oh, I see, you must—"

Like a machine gun, Taiga threw one insult at him after another. Then, suddenly, she closed her mouth. This was it—the most frightening moment. She eyed him with one narrowed and ruthless eye, then approached him from below, trying to make him slip and fall. She would intimidate her opponent with the sheer determination she emitted from her body until they couldn't move.

This was the Palmtop Tiger's real power.

"Are you saying you have a *crush* on me?" she said.

"...Dumba—"

"Hmph, of course not! Not even you would be so stupid to overstep yourself that far, or maybe I should say that you don't have the *guts* for it, huh?!"

"...Ah... Uh..." He was so scared he didn't see the smirk forming on her lips. He returned her glare and desperately tried to shout something. "Of course not!"

Yeah, of *course* not. If love were the feeling he felt toward Minori, then this was a different emotion.

There was one thing Ryuuji was sure of, though. He wanted to take care of Taiga—this Palmtop Tiger. Even if what he felt was different from love, he wanted to be by her side. While he was next to her, he wanted to become that kind of guy. That was it. And it was enough, right? Was it wrong for him to want that?

"...Damn it!" he said. "We're going to the supermarket! And we're buying pork!"

He set out, taking long, resolute strides and huffing with determination.

Their lives would continue on. They had more than enough time. So, this was enough; he had made his mind up. He wasn't going to think about the hard stuff. Right now, the menu was more important.

"If we find good pork today, how about we make pork shabu shabu?" he said. "Oh, but what about a simple grilled pork...? Hey, why aren't you coming?!"

He had kept up his brisk pace as he spoke, but upon noticing that Taiga wasn't following, he made a U-turn.

"Hurry up and come," he urged her. Naturally, he didn't take her hand—instead, he just poked her elbow with the corner of his bag.

"Ryuuji...I want a yogurt parfait."

"Huh? Wh-what, you want to go to the family restaurant instead? Just when I got into the mood for making stuff."

"After that, we'll have pork. With fried ginger—no, a stew, of course. Make sure it's actually creamy."

"What? Stew is fine, but would we have any room left for it? It's already five. We always have dinner before six thirty at my house... Hey, don't ignore me! Why are you walking ahead of me?"

"...Hey. Ryuuji."

Taiga, who had started walking ahead of him of her own accord, suddenly stopped and turned around. Her transparent gaze passed through him. Involuntarily, he tripped up on his words.

"...What is it, T... Taiga?"

237

He became flustered again and cast his gaze toward the twilight sky.

"Can't you shut up for a bit?"

Her terrible words made him doubt his own ears. They bore through him. Before Ryuuji's eyes, Taiga sighed purposefully.

"Right now, I'm heartbroken. You can at least understand that, right? Aren't you even a little worried about me? Of course, you'll help me come up with the next plan, right? Because I'm not giving up on Kitamura-kun after such a small setback! Also, what were you going on about just now? That you're a dragon? Well, I don't care whether you're a dragon or a dog. If you're gonna stay by me like you said, then you better work just as hard to make me happy."

Where did those tears from earlier go? he wondered. The Palmtop Tiger really was the Palmtop Tiger. She toyed with his heart like it was nothing, with spiteful words and a tormenting gaze.

Just how sharp were those claws and teeth of hers? She was bad-tempered, ferocious—just how far would this palmtop-sized, man-eating tiger go to get her way?

Moreover, what kind of fate awaited the one who claimed he would stick beside her?

"M... maybe I acted rashly..." Without thinking, Ryuuji raised his voice and groaned. He stood there, motionless. It was possible he had just made a mistake. He remained in that spot, deep in thought, with both his eyes firmly closed—and because of that, he missed it.

A bit farther off, Taiga was watching Ryuuji. Then, she looked down and smiled.

"...He called me 'Taiga'..."

Butterflies fluttered in her stomach, until finally, like the cooing of a diminutive dove, a laugh transformed her unseen face.

Even to this day, no one in the world has seen it.

Afterword

MOMENT BY MOMENT, I'm packing on more pounds—TakeYuyu, here. These days, the pudge around my waist is pregnant with a sense of urgency, and each time I look at it, I realize anew: *This isn't just a stomach anymore, but a belly.* But, what if that belly is full of hope? What if it's full of dreams? What if it's full of smiles—what then? Right? If it's that kind of belly...then the bigger the better, right? If you don't say yes, then I don't know what will happen to me! (Out of the corner of my eye, I'm staring intensely at an unopened pack of Donbei instant noodles...)

Well then, did you enjoy the first volume of *Toradora!*? To all those who picked it up, I thank you so, so much! If you enjoyed it even a little bit, I'm happy.

Q: I didn't see any parts with battles, or worldbuilding, or anything that really fired me up—what gives?

A: That's by design.

Toradora's world is meant to feel like one of those completely ordinary slice-of-life stories. It's a plain and simple romcom, and I plan on continuing to make it light and fluffy. Please, please, please stick around for the continuation of *Toradora*. You are absolutely more than welcome to.

One more thing—your readership allowed me to write a series called *Our Dear Tamura-kun*, and I wanted to thank all those who sent me their thoughts about it in the mail! I read all of them, and they are very important to me. I want to fall asleep hugging each and every one of them—the letters and I are in a serious relationship. In response to receiving all those voices of support, I intend to work hard so that I can tell you about new developments regarding *Tamura-kun*.

Incidentally, I anticipate this book will reach your hands in March 2006 (or rather than anticipate, plan...). However, I'm writing this afterword today, on January 3rd. Happy New Year! In the first week of the new year, I'm bulldozing through and declaring just one New Year's resolution, which is to strive towards finishing a mountain of work.

I chose this goal because of something Mr. Manager unintentionally said to me.

"...What do you normally do, Takemiya-san?"

I think the person who said that has forgotten all about it, but since it was said to me, I've really opened my eyes. Just...what *do* I do, normally? I'm a full-time housewife—I'm not even working part-time...

While I was thinking about why I got asked that in the first place, eventually, I imagined hearing a fuller version of the question, with the parts Mr. Manager hadn't said out loud.

"(Even though you're new to it, publishing two volumes in one year and having only one draft in the works while being a housewife doesn't seem like a lot of work. As a person who is part of society and should be working,) what do you normally do (outside of work), Takemiya-san? (Also, have you gained weight recently?)"

And then I came back to my senses.

What was I doing normally? I did work, actually, but I was spending a lot more of my time eating snacks, boiling pasta, warming up milk, dressing the pasta and tarako roe, steaming potatoes, putting seaweed on tarako spaghetti, cooking pork belly, putting natto on tarako spaghetti and, well—I was doing all kinds of things like that. Speaking of which...wasn't I eating way too much tarako spaghetti...?

Yes, I stopped the hand that was twirling my tarako spaghetti. I needed to do work more befitting a member of society. It wasn't the time to eat two meals of tarako spaghetti a day (let alone 200 grams of it). Because of that, my stomach has become like this...! If I could only shave off these pounds...!

So, because of that, this year, I'm pushing forward on work. I'm also thinking of cutting back on the tarako spaghetti. Anyway, in order to give you, my readers, tons more to enjoy, I will earnestly and wholeheartedly work so hard that I smash my keyboard to bits.

And I'll also pray that as a result of my hard work, my body will hopefully shape up, too. Please, never again may I have a tragedy where I have to ask to change seats, because I sat down and found my jeans constricting the stomach fat on my waist to the point that it was extremely painful—even after bothering the editorial department for sofa recommendations...

All that said, I'd like to give my thanks to those who read this far. Yasu-chan, who has been in charge of doing the illustrations ever since my previous work, I look forward to continuing to work with you, as well as with my manager.

In order to meet you again in the second volume of *Toradora!*, I'll pick up the pieces of my smashed keyboard at full speed.

—Yuyuko Takemiya

Artist's AFTERWORD

NICE TO MEET YOU. To those who know me, it's nice seeing you again. I'm Yasu. After my previous work for *Our Dear Tamura-kun*, I'm now in charge of the illustrations in *Toradora!*

I thought that *Tamura-kun* would probably be the first and last big job of my life, so when I heard about this current project, I was really shocked. I thought it was someone playing a joke on me. Thank you so much for allowing me to draw for it.

It's been very cold lately, hasn't it? Where I live, we've even gotten snow a few times. I'm bad with snow on account of the cold, but I still kind of want to have a snowball fight. Really though, I just want to play. But it ended up being so cold at home that I couldn't help it—I turned on the heat, so my electric bill was a joke...

Anyway, I have these messages for those I'm indebted to:

- **To Takemiya-sensei**—Thank you for allowing me to have a lot of fun reading through your work this time, too. I rarely eat spaghetti, so next time I'll have some tarako spaghetti.

- **To the editorial department**—I am so very sorry for causing you trouble with my inexperience and slow replies. For the next project, I'm going to work hard to make sure I give myself a little more time. Though, that's probably a fleeting fantasy. (Hey!)

■ **To Ishi-san (who helped me), and also Daiyama-sensei—**
You two always take care of me. Thanks in advance for the
next time, too! (Hey!)

■ **To those who picked up this book and to those who
cheered me on through my website**—Really, thank you so
much. I'm really sorry for all the delays with my replies.

And so, with that, I'm much obliged to all of you again. I
hope you enjoy *Toradora!* >ω<ノ

—Yasu